ON HIS MAJESTY'S
SECRET SERVICE.

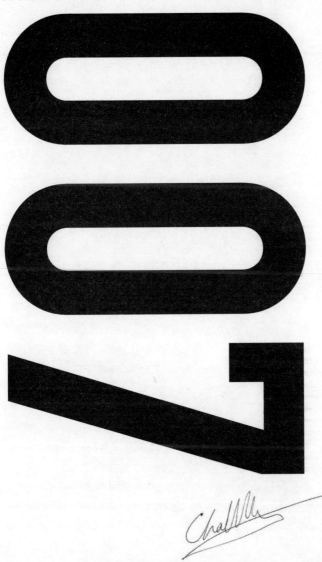

On His Majesty's Secret Service

On His Majesty's Secret Service

First published in Great Britain by Ian Fleming Publications in 2023
Registered offices: 73-74 Berwick Street, London W1F 8TE

www.ianfleming.com

001

Print ISBN: 978-1-915797-11-7
eBook ISBN: 978-1-915797-08-7

A catalogue record for this book is available from the British Library

Typeset by Palimpsest Book Production Ltd, Falkirk, Stirlingshire

Printed and bound in the UK using 100% renewable
electricity by CPI Group (UK) Ltd

MIX
Paper | Supporting
responsible forestry
FSC
www.fsc.org
FSC® C171272

On
His Majesty's
Secret Service

CHARLIE HIGSON

IAN FLEMING PUBLICATIONS

Contents

May 4th – 2 days to the Coronation

Bond's steady, blue eyes were fixed on the spinning blur of silver. It hung in the air like a spent cartridge spat out by a handgun, and then, as quickly as it had gone up, it came down.

As it did so he switched his focus to the man standing over by the chapel windows and let the gleaming circle of metal drop out of his vision and land in his palm with a tiny slap. Swiftly, he inverted his hand and flipped the almost weightless disc onto the back of his other hand.

Now he glanced down.

Heads.

He studied the image on the coin, familiar and yet unfamiliar, and then looked back over to the bank of tall windows where an identical silhouette stood out against the bright, diffused early morning sunlight.

A freshly minted fifty pence piece.

And a not so freshly minted new monarch.

The elderly tweed suit standing next to Bond gave a

1

small tut. *Not done to be tossing coins in the presence of royalty on such a grand occasion, old boy.* Bond turned and smiled at him. Just enough of a smile, tinged with an edge of warning.

The suit saw a man in his mid-thirties. Tall, but compactly built. A stray lock of hair falling casually over his forehead like a black comma. The hint of a scar on his right cheek. Cold, unblinking eyes that offered no promise of comradeship.

And that weaponised smile.

Bond lifted the coin between thumb and forefinger. Then, performing a magician's sleight of hand, it was gone, his smile disappearing along with it. He put the old man out of his mind and shifted his gaze back to Charles, who was at the centre of a small group of people. Specially invited guests. Privileged to be here for the coronation rehearsal in the Abbey. But not quite privileged enough to be invited to the main ceremony in two days' time.

The rehearsal wasn't due to start for another hour, but Charles had to fulfil his royal duties beforehand. He'd be spending the rest of his days shaking hands and trying to summon up small talk. Today was no different.

Even though the walls and windows of the Lady Chapel went up and up and up to an extraordinary, vaulted ceiling of carved stonework, the space felt crowded. The tiled floor crowded with people. And crowded with objects – monuments, statues, tombs. This building was the graveyard of kings. There were thirty monarchs buried here. And not all of them could have been sleeping peacefully. Many had battled, murdered, connived and usurped their way into these royal coffins. Kicking other claimants off the throne. Bond had his back to the tomb of Henry VII – the man who'd had this extension to the eastern end of the Abbey built, eight hundred years ago. Hadn't Henry killed Richard III at the battle of Bosworth, snatched up his crown from a thornbush and brought the upstart Tudor family to the throne?

This place was so stuffed with history that it was hard to concentrate. Everywhere you looked was another painting, another elaborate pillar, another effigy of a dead grandee lying with his feet pointing towards the roof. But Bond tried to shut all that out as he appraised each of the king's guests in turn, his gaze missing nothing, searching for anything that felt wrong, that smelled of a threat, and then, finally, he moved on to Charles's own entourage. Two discreet bodyguards. Various aides and equerries. The efficient young woman with a French braid who never left the King's side, quietly murmuring in his ear and briefing him on the hoof . . .

'This is Sir Norman Bigwig from the Board of Trade . . . Margaret so-and-so from such-and-such a charity . . .'

The young woman was called Rose, or Flora, or Jacinta. Something botanical. M had sent Bond on a crash course in regal etiquette, history and the structure of the royal household, but he was still struggling to work out exactly who everyone was and what exactly they did.

Which one was it? Which one of them was going to betray their monarch?

He discreetly pulled back his right sleeve just enough to show the face of his Rolex. 8.22. He had twenty-six minutes. Twenty-six minutes to figure out who the traitor was.

And he had precious little to go on.

He thought back to how this had all begun. Maybe if he went over the details one more time, he'd spot the one he'd missed. He ran through the events of the previous few weeks like a film in his head. Reviewing every moment . . .

Like so many missions before, it had started when he walked through the heavy, reinforced door into Moneypenny's office and took in the familiar scene. Moneypenny sitting at her desk, unruffled and crisp as ever. He was relieved he didn't have to go through the customary banter with her. Not appropriate this morning. An agent had been killed in Hungary; a fellow Double O. Bond knew that Moneypenny had been seeing him. Not strictly allowed, but it happened.

009. Easier not to give him a name. Besides, Bond had found the man deathly dull. He may have had the moody features of an aftershave model, with manicured stubble to match – the classic 'tall, dark and handsome' package that women were supposed to go nuts for – but that was the end of it. Underneath it all, the man was

4

a stuffed Charles Tyrwhitt shirt. Other agents had been known to walk up several flights of stairs to avoid being stuck in the lift with him.

As far as anyone in the Double O section could be called a safe bet, 009 was just that. Or at least he *had* been. Like a lot of safe bets, it had ended in tears. Not that Moneypenny would ever let anyone see her cry. Never show any weakness. Any girlish emotions. She was a professional.

Bond simply nodded to her, and she nodded back.

She said one word. 'James.'

He replied with one word of his own. 'Moneypenny.'

That said it all.

The green light went on over M's door. He pushed it open and went through.

Another familiar scene. M sitting at his desk, studying some documents. Didn't hold with screens and emails. Didn't trust the digital world – too leaky. You couldn't hack a sheaf of hand-typed paper.

He kept his eyes on the file and didn't look up as Bond came in and quietly closed the door.

'Sit down, 007.'

James sat and waited. He'd left a soft bed and a warm pair of arms to be here, but he felt no regrets. No tiredness. Like a modern sports car, he always started first time, even on a cold morning like today. At last, the old man straightened the papers on his desktop, leaned back in his chair and fixed Bond with his penetrating, grey eyes. Eyes that never aged.

'You've heard?'

'How bad is it, sir?'

'As bad as it could be. Do you know the details of the case?'

'I'm officially on leave, sir. It wasn't exactly a stag weekend in Syria. I've been trying to clear my head of any MI6 matters . . .'

'Yes, all right, I don't need your blog, Bond. A simple "no" would have sufficed.'

'In that case, "no",' said Bond.

'That's better. There's this chap, calls himself Æthelstan of Wessex . . .' He slid a folder over to Bond, who opened it and looked at a photograph that might have been taken in Victorian times. A 50-something man was dressed in what looked like medieval robes, clutching a drinking horn in a hand that was heavy with rings. He had an ostentatious walrus moustache and an extravagant mane of grey hair, held back by some kind of jewelled circlet.

'Claims to be a direct descendent of King Alfred the Great.'

Bond couldn't suppress a snort of laughter.

'Has something amused you, Bond?'

'Alfred had five or six children, sir, and history tells us his lineage carried forward. He's about, what, some thousand years removed from today? Which is, say, about 40 generations or so. Most people living today have somewhere in the region of a trillion ancestors of the 40th generation, give or take a few. So, if you're European, it's likely that Alfred's one of those trillion ancestors. You and me, too, sir. We're all descendants of Alfred the Great.'

'A trillion, Bond? Are you sure about that? That's more people than have ever lived on the planet.'

'Yes. That's just a mathematical model, sir. In real life there's a lot of intermingling, overlapping – cousins marrying cousins, or whatever. It's all folded in. So, the same ancestors will appear over and over again in your one trillion.'

'You don't have to be such a know-it-all, 007.'

'Can't help it, sir.'

'Yes, well that's all well and good, but Wessex has a bona fide family tree, apparently. Very proud of it. Proof of *direct* lineage. A clear, straight line on the male side. As a result, he's got the idea that the wrong man's going to be crowned in May.'

'He's not alone. The world's full of crackpots.'

'And it's our job, Bond, to make sure that none of them gets out of their padded cell and scares the public.'

'How serious a threat is he?'

'Serious enough to have you sitting there. Where 009 sat not too long ago.'

'I see. Yes.'

'The difference with this crackpot is that he has money, he has arms, and he has the men to use them.'

'Seriously?'

M gave Bond a look that said, 'You know me, 007 – I'm always serious.'

Bond pressed on. 'Yes, but what I mean is, sir – surely this man can't have put together a big enough army to pose a significant threat to the UK . . .'

'That's the thing.' M slapped the table. Irritated and ill-at ease. It had been 16 years since the government had banned smoking in offices, but M still resented it.

'The man's not an idiot,' he pressed on. 'Much as he looks like one. He must be at least half mad, yet not so completely deranged that he hasn't amassed a small fortune and put this thing together. He must know that a military coup in England is out of the question. If our friend Putin can't make headway in the Ukraine with the entire might of the Russian military at his disposal, what chance does *Æthelstan of Wessex* have with a small, private army? No matter how well-trained and equipped.'

'So, you think there's something else at play?'

'Has to be. Trying to get any of his men *anywhere near* the king would be nigh on impossible. Particularly with the current levels of security. But it wouldn't look good, would it? To have fireworks on the streets of London on the big day? Blood flowing into the gutters? And at least an *attempt* on the new king's life? Not a good start at all.'

'I take your point.'

'This coronation is a chance to advertise UKplc to the world, Bond. Show the doubters who've written us off that we're open for business. Show them that there are still *some* things we're good at. Like marching bands and bagpipes and knowing how to wear an elaborate hat. The powers that be want to present this country as a safe pair of hands. With age-old traditions and protocol, stability and calm, and the required skillset to form an orderly crowd. And the Windsors want to present the image that everybody loves and supports them. Nothing must spoil this glorious pageant of Merrie England. If the coronation descends into chaos, it leaves doors open for disruptors like Æthelstan.'

Bond studied the photograph in the file again. Looked into the face of the man staring back at him, trying to read a deeper message. He had slightly bulging eyes, open wide enough to show a ring of white around the pupils. Hinting at a thyroid problem. His mouth was gaping in a froglike grin, displaying all the fake bonhomie of a pub bore. But look more closely at the eyes and they display no joy or humour, no merriment, only a pitiless, cold psychopathy.

'Any idea what his wider agenda might be?'

'That's what 009 was trying to find out. What else this clown might be up to. Wessex's base of operations is a castle in Hungary. 009 got in without a hitch, but it seems he slipped up.'

Bond knew that the folder would brief him on all that he needed to know, but he was in a hurry, and M was good at cutting to the point.

'How far did he get, sir?' he asked. 'What happened to him?'

'He got as far as a popular climbing spot in the Zemplen mountains in northern Hungary. Near the border with Slovakia. He was found early one morning at the bottom of a crag. Dressed for a climb. Every bone in his body broken. Bruised all over. An almost lethal amount of alcohol in his blood and, of course, nothing of any interest on him. Just enough in his wallet to make it real.'

Bond let his breath out in a long sigh. It could so easily have been him lying at the foot of that cliff and 009 sitting here with M. He'd lost count of the number of times he'd barely scraped through, survived by the skin of his teeth.

009's luck had run out.

M pointed at the file in Bond's lap.

'009 almost made it out. He knew Æthelstan was on to him and he was just able to send a D37.'

Bond didn't like the codewords and acronyms that were increasingly creeping into the MI6 vocabulary. He felt they were designed to soften the harsh reality of what they did. D37. Looked harmless. But it was a desperate thing. An emergency flare. A shout for help. A dying scream for your mother. No content. Just a digital bleep that communicates when an agent has important information but knows they won't be able to parachute out with it.

Bond flipped through to a map, and then a photograph of a Hungarian castle. A white, stone building on top of a wooded hill, overlooking a wide, forested valley.

'Szalkai Castle,' said M. 'Known by the locals as "*Az ördög széke*" – the devil's seat.'

Bond raised an eyebrow. 'And you want me to get in there?'

'I'm afraid I do. This is very sensitive, Bond. We can't leave this to any other agency, and we can't get the Hungarians involved. They're evidently protecting the man. We have to handle it ourselves. With the minimum of fuss.' M held Bond's gaze. 'If you were 009, what would you have done? If you knew they were onto you? What would you have done with your information?'

'I'd have concealed it somewhere in the castle.'

'That's just what I thought. If you can get in there and find it quickly, you'll save yourself a lot of leg work, going over the same ground as 009.'

'But if they already know we're onto them . . .' said Bond, studying the map and drumming on the arm of his chair. A grunt from M made him look up. The old man was giving his restless fingers a hard stare. Bond stilled them.

'I can offer you the same backup as 009 had. And more. Whatever you need to get in there and stop this man, in whatever way you see fit.'

'Whatever way I see fit?'

'Don't make me spell it out, James. We both know what your Double O prefix means. There's a mad dog that needs to be quietly put down and buried before it bites too many people.'

Bond nodded and stood up. He would read the file properly at his desk. He walked towards the door but stopped and turned back before opening it.

'Forgive my impertinence, sir . . .'

'Out with it.'

'You have always stressed that *exercising* my licensed rights should only ever be a last resort.'

'This is different,' said M quietly. 'That woman in the outer office.' He nodded to the door. 'Who has sat there, year after year, asking for nothing. She offered her resignation recently.'

'Moneypenny?' Bond could hardly believe it.

'009, too . . . As you know, agents can't marry within the service. But she and he . . .'

11

M made a vague gesture and left the rest of the sentence hanging.

'I'm not given to sentimentality, James, but I don't think it would be overstating the case if I said I loved that girl, dearly.'

'I understand.' Bond *did* understand. He also understood that nobody within the service would ever hand in their resignation to marry him.

He was not the marrying kind.

March 7th – 60 days
until the Coronation

The Croatian section of the Adriatic Highway that runs between Makarska and Ravca is one of the great drives of the world. A two-lane highway with dramatic, rocky slopes on one side and a sheer drop to the deep blue sea on the other.

Not that any of this registered with Marina Buehler, who was sitting in the back of a cream Bentley Continental, scrolling through Instagram pictures of spectacular beauty spots around the world, barely glancing out of the window. They'd set off early from Dubrovnik to avoid the traffic and the road was largely clear. With any luck they'd be in Makarska before 11a.m. She could enjoy a coffee at one of the places around the harbour, and then she could hop on board the *Lady Ealhswith*, ready to set sail for Venice before lunch.

She'd spent the night in Dubrovnik, where she'd been attending the opening of an exhibition of photographs of refugees at a strange gallery that was part exhibition space and part high-end clothing boutique. The huge black and white images of frightened people with drawn faces hanging among the expensive frocks was a jarring juxtaposition. It had been a big society event, sponsored by an Austrian friend with contacts in high places. Marina had little interest in photography, and even less in refugees, but she was very interested in being photographed. She'd spent the first hour of the drive scrutinising pictures from last night, making sure she looked good.

She was satisfied.

She kept her attention on her screen, shutting herself off from the world. She had no inclination to look at the Adriatic. She'd see enough of that on the voyage to Venice. The charming array of the Split islands, lifting their heads above the water? Boring. And she had no wish to engage in conversation with the two men sitting in the front of the car. Her driver, Giorgio, and her bodyguard, Carl. As ever they were talking about football. The capacity for men to talk for an interminable length about football always amazed her. Her husband was no exception. He liked nothing more than to settle down with a pint of beer with 'the lads' and watch a game. She couldn't see that there was that much to say. If one team scored more goals than the other, they won. That was all there was to it. What was the point of going any deeper into a discussion on the subject?

But now Marina became aware of a change in mood, and she tore her eyes from the screen. Carl was twisted around in his seat, staring out of the back window with a strained look on his face.

'What are these clowns playing at?'

As he said it, there was a deep roar and a motorbike overtook them on a bend.

'What a dick,' Carl muttered and turned back to face front.

The motorbike had slowed to a crawl in the middle of the road in front of them. There was no way Giorgio could get past. Marina saw Carl's eyes flick to the rear-view mirror and now she turned round to see what he was looking at. Two more motorbikes. The riders wearing padded leather jackets and full-face helmets.

'This is not a road for playing games on,' said Giorgio. 'But he is going so slow.'

The next moment, the bike in front of them slewed round in the road. Giorgio shouted in shock and stamped on the brake pedal. They skidded and squealed to a juddering halt, accompanied by a tirade of colourful Italian from Giorgio, stopping just centimetres short of the bike. All three of them were thrown forward against their seat belts, but the stop hadn't been abrupt enough to trigger the airbags. The bike rider had timed it perfectly.

In all the time that he'd worked for Marina and her husband, Carl had never had to actually do anything. As Marina understood it, he was more of a deterrent than anything else. And now, he'd been so taken by surprise, his reactions were slow and clumsy. He was still struggling to pull his gun from inside his jacket and get out of the car when a second bike pulled level with his door and the rider grabbed him by the collar. The next moment he was sprawled on the tarmac with a pistol jammed into the side of his neck.

Marina gave a small, involuntary shriek as the third rider appeared. He ran to Carl, grabbed him by the arm and he and his accomplice hauled him to his feet, manhandled him across the road and tossed him over the crash barrier.

Marina put a hand to her mouth. This was unreal. A scene from a movie. She couldn't believe it was actually happening to her.

The rider who had stopped in front of them had come to the car and was leaning over with one knee on the front passenger seat, jamming a stubby, black handgun into Giorgio's neck, just below his ear. So hard that Giorgio's head was pressed against the side window. He was wide-eyed. Sweating. Repeating 'no-no-no-no-no . . .' over and over.

The other two men had returned. One gestured to Marina with his gun hand.

'Out.'

She did as was she was told. In a daze. Like an automaton. She could see that, thank God, the slope wasn't as steep here as in other places. Carl had rolled down only about 10 metres and become entangled in a clump of small pine trees and rugged coastal shrubs.

She looked at the riders, their faces partially obscured by the visors of their helmets. They looked like locals, but could equally be Turkish or Albanian. One of them snatched her bag off the back seat. Her chain-strap Prada. The bag itself was probably worth more than the contents. He then plucked her phone out of her hand. She hadn't even realised she was still holding it. She felt suddenly naked and helpless without it.

'Please . . .' she said limply.

'Give me the bracelets. Your watch. Do it. Now.'

Marina was shaking, starting to panic; even the tiniest action seemed impossibly hard work. She fumbled with her watch fastening, the men glaring at her impatiently.

Then there was a confusion of noise and movement. Everything happening too fast and all at once, so that she couldn't keep up. A car came thundering up from the opposite direction. The driver saw the motorbike blocking the road and managed to slow down just enough and swerve so that it merely clipped the front wheel of the bike, knocking it over. The two riders in the road had to jump clear, one of them slipping over and tumbling onto the tarmac. The car came to a rest on the wrong side of the road.

Oh no, Marina thought. Somebody else is going to get hurt now.

The three riders started shouting to each other and in the next moment the new driver was out of the car and moving quickly. He was smartly dressed in a suit and tie, but looked fiercely determined. Perhaps he'd meant to knock the motorbike over after all. He ran forward in a crouch, keeping his shoulders low, and barrelled into the rider who was still standing before he was able to fire off a shot.

Now the rider with one knee on the passenger seat and one foot on the road, came to life. He twisted round and tried to get out of the car. But the man in the suit was ready for him. In one deft movement he spun round and slammed the door in the man's face. He yelled and

17

fell back. The driver continued his spin and launched himself at the man who had first gone down, kicking him hard in the chest just as he struggled to his feet. The rider fell back heavily, his helmet thumping onto the ground.

The man in the suit moved with athletic grace, scooping up a fallen handgun and checking it quickly before firing it into the air. This got the attention of the three riders. They scrambled to get away, dashing for their bikes. The one that been knocked over was evidently not damaged too much. Its rider hauled it upright and kicked it into life as he jumped into the saddle. In a matter of seconds, they were gone, back the way they'd come, leaving a blue haze of fumes and a ringing in Marina's ears.

As quickly as it had started, it was over.

The driver walked to the Bentley. 'Are you all right, Ma'am?'

Marina hadn't expected him to have an English accent.

'Yes . . . No . . . I think so . . . I don't know . . . They took my bag. My phone.'

'Could have been a lot worse.' He gave her a re-assuring smile. She saw now that he was rather good-looking. Or was she projecting that onto him? Already personifying him as her handsome saviour. Her dashing knight in shining armour.

He had the polite, formal air of someone used to being in control. A policeman, or a soldier. An officer. An officer and a gentleman.

He looked away down the road. 'If I'd been thinking

on my feet, I'd have memorised a license plate number. Although the bikes were probably stolen.' He smiled at her again. 'It's lucky I came along when I did. Ironically, I'm on my way to a security conference in Dubrovnik. My line of work. There's been rather a lot of this sort of thing happening round here lately. It's getting worse. Carjacking. Mugging. People being robbed at gunpoint. Now, I'd better move my car before I cause an accident.'

Giorgio had got out of the Bentley, shaking and muttering saints' names to himself. He climbed over the crash barrier and went down to help Carl.

The Englishman put a hand on Marina's arm. 'Will you be all right?'

Marina nodded, suddenly unable to speak. Tears were welling behind her eyes. Her throat was tight. She felt pathetically grateful to this man.

At last, she managed to choke some words out. 'Can I give you a reward in some way? I'd like to thank you . . .'

'Don't worry about it. This is what I do.'

'Will you tell me your name, at least?'

'Of course. The name's Sanbourne. Peter Sanbourne.'

He fished a card out of his wallet and passed it to her. 'If you ever want to upgrade your security to a level that . . .' He looked at the Bentley, and then over the crash barriers to where Giorgio and Carl were noisily climbing back up. '*To a level that actually works*. Just get in touch.'

And with that he walked over to his car, climbed in and drove away.

March 23rd – 44 days
until the Coronation

Bond was eating a breakfast of plain yoghurt topped with fruit and berries, followed by two eggs, scrambled, on wholemeal toast. A plain, functional breakfast in a plain, functional hotel. Clean and modern, with that indefinable civilised Continental feel to it. What in England would have been characterless and bland – a Premier Inn, or a Travelodge – here, in Budapest, felt somehow sophisticated and chic in its efficient simplicity.

As he ate, he studied a fifty pence piece on the tabletop. He rarely carried change these days but had bought a coffee at Heathrow with a five pound note and had been shocked to see how little change he'd been given. He hadn't given the piece a second glance at the time, but when he was emptying everything he'd deemed unnecessary for the day from his pockets before coming down to breakfast, he'd spotted that the distinctive seven-sided coin had the profile of King Charles on it. These coins had been in circulation since the end of last year, but it was the first one he'd seen. Charles was facing left, the opposite direction to Queen Elizabeth. The reverse of the coin showed four royal shields, representing the four home nations, the English one with the quarters of the royal arms depicted within it. In between each shield was an emblem of a rose, a thistle, a shamrock and a leek. England, Scotland, Northern Ireland and Wales.

What a lot of history this simple design represented.

Bond turned it back over. The portrait of Charles made him look old. He *was* old. It was just his luck to finally make it onto British coins and stamps just as people were no longer using cash or sending letters.

Bond scooped the last spoonful of yoghurt into his mouth and moved onto his eggs.

Back in the day he'd have gone for the full, expense account blowout. In a British hotel that meant a 'Full English' and in a European one like this, cold meats, cheese, pastries, croissants . . . but he'd learned that he functioned better with a lighter load, and he'd read an interesting article on the flight over in a copy of *New Scientist* he'd picked up at the airport. The article was about new research into gut health. How it was important to nurture the bacteria in your intestines, to feed the good flora and fauna, the tiny, teeming microbes that lived inside you, and to discourage the bad ones, with a mixed diet. You needed to eat plenty of fibre, varied fruit and vegetables and fermented foods like yoghurt, kimchi and kombucha.

Normally he might had dismissed all this as food faddishness, but what had struck him forcibly was that

21

having gut feelings was a real thing, apparently. The human gut is a very primitive nervous system all of its own. It sends signals to the brain and the brain sends messages back. An unhealthy gut could lead to depression and stress. And vice versa. It was a closed feedback loop.

As a man who relied on gut sense to stay alive, Bond had paid close attention to the article. He lived an inherently unhealthy lifestyle, in as much as there was the ever-present chance of being violently killed. If eating properly gave him an edge, then he wasn't going to argue with the article's findings. He knew his gut wasn't in the best condition. He'd been stabbed in the belly once and had a section of his colon removed.

The rhythms of his life were totally unhealthy, too. Long, tedious periods of nothing happening, followed by brief periods of intense, dangerous activity. Inevitably, after every mission, he'd sink into a depression as his energy levels dropped. The only thing that helped was driving hard, playing hard – squash, tennis, running, swimming – distracting himself with drink and women and gambling. All the while waiting for the real distraction he needed. Another mission.

As he got older, there was always the danger of slowing down. Of losing his sensitivity to threat. Of losing his *gut sense*. That primitive, unconscious, unreasoning, reactive gut level of intelligence that would make him fire off a round a split second before his enemy.

He finished his meal with a cup of jet-black coffee and went out to see what the day had to offer. He was wearing a lightweight, knee-length, charcoal grey, woollen overcoat, and a quarter-zip, merino top in a paler shade of grey over a plain white t-shirt. Black trousers and a pair of black desert boots completed his outfit. Monochrome, anonymous, practical. Smart without being showy.

He favoured classic men's tailoring. Clothing that was built to hold its shape and last without shouting 'look at me'. He had to be able to move easily and not be concerned about whether the seams were going to hold up if he got into a scrape. And he rejected anything with an obvious logo. He was damned if he was going to be a walking advertisement for some multinational clothing brand who had their stuff made in a sweatshop by children paid in pennies.

When he left the hotel, he walked briskly down to the nearby intersection, turned left and walked a little way along the road before crossing to the tram stop in the centre. Bond liked Budapest. It was largely unspoilt and had an air of civilised calm and self-worth.

He had a map of the city centre memorised in his head, along with a basic overview of tram routes, bus routes and Metro lines. It helped that this wasn't his first time in Budapest, and, when revisiting a city he knew well, the details came back to him easily. It was just one of the many skills he'd picked up in the service.

The tram rails ran down the centre of the main roads. It was a well-organised service, reflecting the ordered efficiency of the city in general. So different to the noisy, crowded, confusing, impatient bustle of London. Bond supposed that that was the difference between a city of one and a quarter million people, and a city of nearly 10 million people, like London. Mumbai, in India, was something else again. Twelve million people, and with such a sense of dizzy, seething, chaotic humanity that all you could do was give into it and be swept up by the sense of exhilarating madness.

Here, locals waited patiently for the next tram, secure in the knowledge that one would be along soon. Sure enough, Bond was there for less than two minutes before a long, yellow, number 2 tram arrived.

He climbed aboard the last carriage and made sure to stand at the back. The three jointed carriages had no dividers between them, so he had an uninterrupted view down the length of the vehicle. A harassed young mother got on after him, holding an angry toddler against her chest, trying to subdue him as he furiously wriggled, red-faced and bellowing. She had limp, greasy hair and a tatty old coat. Bond moved to stand as close to her as he could without invading her space. If anyone was tailing him, they wouldn't have got on through the same doors as him, which meant, as he faced the front of the tram, they would be ahead of him. Close enough to keep an eye on him. Almost everybody on the tram was looking at the squalling boy. Some with only side-long glances, others with affronted glares, as this tiny air raid siren disrupted their peaceful journey. Bond was checking for anyone who didn't look around, because looking round would mean looking directly at Bond. He spotted five of them. A young couple chatting away to each other, oblivious to anyone else on the tram, including the child. An old woman sitting, resolutely staring at nothing. She looked like she'd seen it all and was probably half deaf. The child was no concern of hers. And then there was a thirtysomething young man, too intent on studying his phone to look up, and another, older man, dressed like everyone else in Budapest on this crisp morning, in a black puffer jacket. A scarf around his neck. A knitted cap on his head. A wiry red beard and the misshapen face of a man who'd been in one too many fights, not caring if he lost. He was standing by the next set of doors, holding the railing and staring out of the window, making sure he didn't look over towards Bond. If there was a tail on him, then either of these last two could be it. Bond thought the bruiser by the door, ready to make a fast exit if needed, the most likely.

The tram ran along the Buda side of the Danube for a while, with views over to Pest on the far bank, and then made its way around the extravagant, and faintly ridiculous, Hungarian Parliament Building, which soared up like an ornate, neo-gothic cathedral, festooned with spires and domes, turrets and balconies. Once past the parliament, the tram pressed along through a more non-descript, semi-industrial area.

At the Fővám tér stop near the Freedom Bridge, Bond waited till the doors had almost closed before hopping off. He didn't look back but walked briskly away from the bridge towards the Market building. The frontage had the feel of a grand old station, and the whole edifice gave off an air of civic pride. Bond pushed his way in through hanging plastic flaps and paused for a moment to take in the interior, which was a single vast space, with a high roof held up by ornate iron work.

Metal staircases at the corners led to an upper floor that ran round the edge of the building. Bond knew not to venture up there. It was a migraine-inducing nightmare of glittery tourist tat. Embroidered cloths from China, garish dolls, plastic rubbish, shot glasses, and 'I ♥ Budapest' t-shirts.

The ground floor was taken up by a grid of ornate stalls that had stood here since the 19th century. They sold everything you'd expect to find in a food market – meat and vegetables, cheese, and endless variations of paprika; hot, sweet, smoked, in jars, bottles, paper packages. Bond was amused and a bit saddened by how places like these became parodies of themselves, reduced to selling stereotypical 'traditional' local items.

Most of the people in here were tourists taking and posing for photographs, but there were some older locals buying provisions at the food stalls, which at least kept the place as something more than an indoor Hungarian theme park.

Bond strolled casually, taking a meandering route and stopping now and then to take in the charm and beauty of the old stalls, as innocuous as any tourist.

He'd promised to bring a present back for Yasmin from his 'business trip', something 'typically Hungarian'. This might be his only chance. He didn't think she'd appreciate a Hungarian salami sausage, so, like so many tourists before him, he settled on a packet of paprika. Hot and smoked.

Told himself it was the thought that counted.

Theirs was a casual relationship. He believed the term was 'friends with benefits', although younger people called it a 'situationship'. Well, he and Yasmin were old enough and grown-up enough not to have to call it that. In fact, they didn't have to call it anything. It was what it was. They both understood the parameters without having to discuss it.

They'd agreed not to ask each other about their private lives, but live in a sensuous bubble. He knew enough to know that she was a busy lawyer specialising in immigration law, and that he wasn't the only man she was seeing. She knew enough to know that he did something for the Foreign, Commonwealth & Development Office and had to travel overseas frequently to attend dull meetings and international conferences.

New protocols that M had put in place stipulated that the tech heads in the basement at Regent's Park checked out the personal details of anybody that a Double O agent was seeing regularly. Bond complied, but had told the tech team that, unless they found anything suspicious, they should keep their findings to themselves. It felt intrusive to know any more. Damn it, it *was* intrusive, a form of stalking, but enough spies had made fools of themselves over the years with a pretty girl, or a handsome young man, to make it a necessity. Albeit a secret one.

The tech team also worked round the clock protecting

their agents' identities. If Yasmin had done a Google search on him – and she probably had done (she could afford a scandal no less than him) – she would have found that his cover story was watertight. She might have been surprised and just a little curious to discover that there were no photographs of him anywhere online. But she'd never said anything, and he had a story ready just in case. As someone in the FCDO, he had to keep his head down.

By mutual agreement they took no photographs of each other. Theirs was a private relationship.

So, Bond was faceless online. The tech heads in Regent's Park, toiling away in their windowless dungeon, like the dwarves in one of Tolkien's fantasies, kept going by Diet Coke and Nutella, were constantly scouring the Internet, searching for any photographs of Mister James Bond and removing them. They also carefully monitored and amended any mentions of him.

They had also set up a false identity for Peter Sanbourne, his current alias. Whenever a Double O agent needed an alias, there was one ready for them. The photographs already prepared. James Bond didn't exist online, but Peter Sanbourne, security expert, had a rich and colourful history. If you knew where to look.

There was virtually nothing about him on the 'ordinary web', as befitted someone in his secretive line of work. And there was precious little more on the dark web. But what there was, was very cleverly constructed and nurtured.

Whenever a fresh identity was needed for an agent,

the old identity would be removed from the Internet and the new one installed. Bond didn't know how they did it and didn't care. They probably used AI and algorithms and all that other computer stuff you read about every day. So much of what MI6 did now was in the digital world. It was all about screens and data and hacking. A Double O agent like himself was something of an anachronism, and every year another agent left the service, or died, or was killed like poor 009. Lately they'd mostly stopped being replaced. Outsourcing was a buzz word at MI6, and the use of satellites and drones was increasingly replacing boots on the ground.

But when it came down to it, ultimately, what Bond did couldn't be done by a computer.

It was personal. It was human. It was intimate.

Bond hated it when he got stuck behind a desk between missions. And he hated it when he had to go in for a briefing with the tech heads. He was bored to tears by their PowerPoint demonstrations, spreadsheets, the endless data and graphs, satellite footage, flow charts, lines of code. He just wanted to run screaming from the room and punch something.

Which was lucky, because that's what his job boiled down to.

He was a fist, clenched and ready to strike.

Once he'd done a couple of circuits of the market, he picked up his pace, squeezed through an area congested with gawpers, doubled back, and darted out of a corner door. He was through the hanging plastic screens and out into a busy side street in a moment and then ducked through an archway into the service area of the large building opposite.

It was a bright, clear day, the strong sunlight creating deep shadows so that Bond was well-hidden in the recessed darkness of the service area. The street was busy enough with people to distract the eye of any potential tail, and his own eyes stayed fixed on the exit he had emerged from. Waiting to see which, if any, of the people from the tram might be following him. His money was still on the man in the knitted cap. He would probably have taken his hat off as a simple but effective change of outfit, but, whilst two or three men came out, none was him.

Just then, an attractive young woman emerged. Natural blonde hair, glowing in the sunlight, a wide mouth, sunglasses, and a chic, belted coat. She was a vision, a radiant presence in this non-descript side street. Bond told himself not to be distracted. To keep his mind on the job, and was just about to look away and forget her, when something clicked.

Clever.

This was the young mother on the tram with the toddler. A neat trick. Instead of trying to blend in, she'd made herself so bloody obvious Bond hadn't given her a second look. She'd been hiding in plain sight, knowing that Bond would dismiss her and be distracted by the toddler. Easy enough to hand the child over to an accomplice when she got off the tram – maybe knitted cap? – remove her greasy wig and swap coats. He applauded their ingenuity. They were good.

Just not quite good enough.

Now Bond had permission to study her more closely. She carried herself with confidence and had an athletic build. Her skin was pale, almost luminous. She looked around, annoyed at having lost her quarry, gave a final glance up and down the street, and then headed up to the main road. Once she'd gone a few paces, Bond slipped out of his hiding place and hurried away in the opposite direction. He took a circuitous route to a different tram stop and rode from there a few stops back to the Metro station at the bottom of Andrássy.

This Budapest Metro Line 1 is the oldest electrified subway system in the world, built using the shuttered system, where they'd simply dug down through the street and then boarded over the roof. So that the rickety old carriages from the 1930s ran along more of a trench than a tunnel, with the stations just a few steps down from the street. Bond hopped on a train and grabbed one of the worn, leather straps that hung from the roof, taking a moment to admire the immaculate old tiles on the walls, displaying the station name.

There was no sign of anyone tailing him. He rode the five stops to Opera where he got out and hurried up the steps. He took in the grand old Hungarian Opera House, remembering the time he'd broken an enemy agent's neck during a performance of 'Der Rosenkavalier'. Not the most pleasant memory. The smell of blocked drains and urine came back to him vividly. He made his way north up Andrássy, which ran dead straight all the way up to Hero's Square where the gold statue of the Angel Gabriel stood on its gleaming white column. As he neared his destination, he kept on the lookout for the girl. If she had any sense, she'd have come straight here to be ready for his arrival. Sure enough, he spotted her before she spotted him, her own golden hair as easy to pick out as the statue.

Bond took out his phone, activated one of the apps and waited for the screen to go dark before pressing on. The girl was standing in a shop doorway, and he was able to sneak up on her from behind the screens around some roadworks. Before she knew it, he was walking casually up to her. They locked eyes and he smiled. There was a pleasing moment of confusion in her expression, but she quickly got it under control and gave the briefest of nods to Bond.

'Excuse me,' he said, friendly and relaxed. 'Do you speak English?'

'A little.' The girl had a European accent. Hard to pin down. Possibly Scandinavian.

Bond pulled his phone out of his pocket and waved it at her. 'Do you have the time, please, my phone's died on me.'

The girl had been put on the back foot. She hesitated, then took off her sunglasses, pulled her own phone out and thumbed it awake.

Bond looked at her eyes. Why had he not noticed them on the tram? They were grey, flecked with green and slanted slightly upwards. Witch's eyes. They perfectly suited her face, which had interesting imperfections, so that there was something both ugly and beautiful about her.

'It is seventeen minutes of eleven.'

'Thank you so much.' Bond smiled, put his phone back in his pocket and walked across the street. When the girl woke her phone, it would have transferred all her data onto Bond's via the neat app that the mechanics in Q branch had installed for him. It had been an untraceable and invisible interaction between their devices. A handshake, a bump, a data exchange, whatever you wanted to call it.

Bond thought of it as an intimate, digital pick-pocketing.

He found the discreet door for the 360 Bar, where he was meeting his contact, next to the art nouveau Párizsi Nagyáruház department store. It had been a bookshop when Bond was last here but was now sadly closed. The dedicated lift to take guests up to the rooftop was situated in an anonymous office lobby, with an unmanned reception desk. Nobody else was waiting, so Bond took his phone out, tapped it and brought it up to his face, letting it stare back at him. It had more security than a market town pub on a Friday night. Facial recognition. Retinal recognition. Fingerprint recognition. Without passing all three tests, anyone trying to hack into it would end up at a dummy, false front stuffed with innocuous apps and personal data.

Even if you got past the false front you were confronted with apps that weren't all they seemed. Bond selected a generic photo-editing app and opened it. Three clicks later, he was past the facade and in through the back door. Now the screen was cleared of all bright colours, whizzy graphics and flashing come-ons. In their place was a list of raw data, black text on grey, with a handful of thumbnail photographs. All showing the girl who was right now stationed across the road, her name spelled out at the top of the page.

Ragnheiður Ragnarsdóttir.

Getting to this screen had taken Bond a matter of seconds, but he needed to make his way to the roof as quickly as possible. Ragnheiður would have alerted his contact that he was on his way up. Any delay would look suspicious.

He pressed the call button for the lift with barely a glance and began scrolling down the screen, absorbing as much information as he could. A gun and a fast and powerful pair of fists were useful in his line of work, but knowledge was the deadliest weapon.

Ragnheiður looked different in every photograph. Short hair, long hair, number 2 buzzcut, red wig, blonde wig, pigtails . . . One day she was dressed from head to toe in haute couture, on another it was combat trousers and boots, or bikini, or business suit. She could be punk, goth, country set, nerd, in sunglasses, prescription glasses, and bizarrely, in one picture, she was even wearing a jewelled eye patch.

In some of the photographs she looked quite young. No more than 13 or 14. Which meant that she'd struggled with her identity and self-image and had been trying to disguise herself long before she'd got involved with this current operation. She was a chameleon, but Bond would recognise her in any disguise now. He felt he knew her intimately.

The lift arrived and three young people got out, laughing and chatting. German tourists. He stepped back to let them pass, then got into the lift. Pressing the sole button for the top floor, he waited for the doors to close before returning his attention to his screen.

He moved on past the photographs to the text.

He'd already deduced from her name that she was Icelandic. It explained her hard-to-pin-down features. The slightly elfin quality he'd noticed in some Icelandic women. The wide, piercing eyes with an upward slant. Scandinavian mixed with something more mysterious. A witch. A disir. A shape-shifting Viking sea spirit. A nixie.

By the time he reached the top floor and the doors slid open, revealing a bright blue sky, he'd stitched together a lifetime, his eyes pin-balling from one fact to another. This was his *gut sense* in action, hardly even computing the information with his conscious mind. The plain list of facts told him everything.

Ragnheiður Ragnarsdóttir.

Icelandic.

28 years old.

Official employment: The White Dragon Sovereign Nation Institute. Which described itself as an ethical investment fund. She was listed as a 'consultant' in their Security Subsidiary, The Hauser Consultancy, which Bond supposed went some way to explaining what she was doing skulking around the streets of Budapest with a borrowed toddler.

He'd known too many of her type over the years. Poor little rich girl struggling to find an identity and a meaning to her life, not caring who she hurt to find her own peace of mind. Someone who'd been given everything she needed by her parents, except their love. Mummy and Daddy locked into a destructive, dysfunctional relationship. Mother an ex-model, or a socialite, or perhaps a small-time actress. Daddy something in finance, or a media mogul, or an entrepreneur, building a business empire on inherited wealth.

In this poor little rich girl's case, her mother was indeed a model, and her father, Ragnar Thorbjörnson, was one of the few people in Iceland who'd managed to make something out of the chaos that had erupted like a volcano when the insane financial bubble burst in 2008. A time when Icelandic fishermen had become bankers overnight and everyone was amazed when the Icelandic economy threw itself off a cliff into the North Sea. Ragnar Thorbjörnson was one of the few who'd been able to climb out of the barrel of rotting fish smelling of roses.

Who was it who first said that money can't buy you love? Or happiness. Or a stable upbringing. But it can buy you a lot of drugs and a Lamborghini Gallardo, and a year's stay in a private hospital when you put the two together and drive into a wall at four o'clock in the morning on the Amalfi Coast. A team of expensive plastic surgeons had had to reconstruct her face, which partly explained the fascinating asymmetrical look of her features that gave her that ugly, beautiful aura.

A year in hospital gives you a lot of time to think, a lot of time to reassess your life, and a sharper sense of mortality. When she came out, the shapeshifter sloughed off her empty-headed, socialite skin and emerged as a revolutionary, burning to change the world, seeking out protest groups. Starting soft with Stop the City, Extinction Rebellion, Antifa, and Golden Dawn, but growing ever more extreme, joining smaller, more militant, and more obscure groups. She was unfocused. As long as an organisation was anti something, she was pro it. The more disruptive, the more it got up the noses of her parents and the establishment, the so-called mainstream, the more she enjoyed it. The left-leaning groups, the greens, the eco warriors, proved to be too mild for her tastes, too easily accepted by the hated, soft liberal centrists. She started to seek out the violent groups, which were inevitably on the far right. She swapped the anarchists for the fascists. Getting into white supremacy, nationalism, the Great Replacement.

Bond had always thought that the far right was closer to the far left than it was to the centre. He disliked anybody, and any movement, that was too 'far' in any direction. If that made him bourgeois, if that made him dull and mainstream, then so be it.

He'd spent his life cleaning up the mess these people left and he was sick of it.

He took one last look at Ragnheiður. Wasn't it always

the way that the child who most rebelled in their early years was the one that ended up most like their parents in later life?

Bond stepped out of the lift into bright sunlight and slipped on his Persol aviators.

He was on the roof of the building, which was covered in decking. There was a small, L-shaped bar in the centre, with removable screens for walls. But the most eye-catching feature of the place were eight transparent, heated, plastic domes, like igloos, with seats and tables inside.

Bond made his way to a low perimeter wall and leant on a shelf for resting one's drinks, admiring the view.

By the standards of New York or Dubai, he might as well still be at ground level. No buildings in the city were taller than 96 metres. Which was about eight storeys. Looking around at the view, there was a pleasing and unfamiliar uniformity to the city. None of the views blighted by ostentatious dick-waving skyscrapers. There were no Gherkins, or Shards, or Walkie Talkies here. And you didn't need to go up into the heavens and risk a nosebleed to get an uninterrupted view. Only two buildings stood out above the others – St Stephen's Basilica and the Hungarian Parliament Building. Both completed around the turn of the 19th century. Both the same height: 96 metres.

Bond was looking west towards the river. On the far side was the great castle on a high promontory. Funny how places built to impose military might were now picturesque tourist attractions. To the left of the castle was the Gellért Hill Liberty Statue.

Initially put up by the Soviets just after the war, to celebrate the release of Hungary from German occupation, and its new status as a Soviet satellite state, the statue was of a woman holding a giant palm leaf above her head.

Neither Nazi Germany nor Soviet Russia had been welcome here, though. They were two sides of the same dirty, debased coin. After the Hungarians had kicked out their Soviet overlords, the statue was changed to an all-purpose personification of liberty. And now it celebrated freedom from the whole damned lot of them.

Which is why Bond felt a deep sense of gloom that this beautiful, civilised, orderly country had been dragged back towards the far right by Viktor Orban, using the crude but effective nationalist playbook. Stirring Hungarians up with his anti-Semitic conspiracy theories, and crude, 'Make Hungary Great again', anti-immigration rhetoric. He'd aligned himself with the likes of Trump and Le Pen and Putin, and, just like them, he was using a paper-thin front of Patriotism to mask rampant self-interest.

In this uncertain world, the age-old lure of the Strong Man held an irresistible appeal to all those who felt left behind and bewildered by change.

Bond had no love of autocrats of whatever hue. From what he'd read in M's file, Æthelstan of Wessex was a friend of Orban. It was no coincidence that Æthelstan, whilst purporting to be an arch British patriot, had set up camp, not in some archetypal English town like Royal Tunbridge Wells, or Westward Ho!, or

Stratford-on-Avon, but here, in Hungary, with Orban's blessing. And his protection. There was no way to make an open and overt move against Æthelstan. Which is why Bond was here.

He became aware that someone was standing at his side, leaning over and admiring the same view.

'Budapest is beautiful in the spring.'

Bond hesitated a moment before replying, 'The crocuses are blooming in the churchyard,' and went on gazing at the scenery.

'I'm sorry?'

'Isn't that the code that agents are supposed to say to each other when they meet? Granted, "*Budapest is beautiful in the spring*" is one degree less corny, but, *really*, do we have to go through this bullshit? Your amateur hour tailing operation. Coded greetings. You know who I am. Peter Sanbourne. You've no doubt got a picture of me on your phone. And you're Canner Lyle. I've definitely got a picture of you on mine.'

'I'm not sure I know what you mean, buddy.' Canner Lyle's voice was bland and unconcerned.

Bond sighed and gave the prearranged answer in a weary monotone. 'I hear it can get very humid in the summer.'

'That's better.' This time Canner sounded cold and annoyed. 'You'd have saved us both a lot of time if you'd just given that response straight away.'

Bond knew you shouldn't judge a man by the way he spoke, but Lyle had the type of closed mouth South African accent that he found grating. Besides, he'd already judged Lyle, based on what he'd read in the file.

South African special forces. 'Military Adviser' to Ugandan troops fighting against the ADF. Left the army in murky circumstances, found a modicum of wealth and fame as a cage fighter, and then set up his own 'private security' company in 2019. He was a mercenary in all but job title.

He'd earned himself the nickname 'Canner' when he'd sealed up six ADF insurgents in empty oil drums until they'd volunteered the information he wanted from them. The location of their base in the jungles of the Democratic Republic of Congo.

But not before three of them had died.

He'd sent the drums, with the dead bodies still inside them, to their base, on the back of a truck.

Charming.

'What's the hurry?' said Bond. 'I'm enjoying the view. As you say, Budapest is very beautiful in the spring.'

'Puh. It's not my idea of a city,' said Lyle. 'It's stunted. Stunted and old and boring. You know that no building can stand over 96 metres?'

'I do, actually, yes.'

'You know why they chose that height? The number 96 has symbolic value in this country. Hungarian Magyars first came here in 896. They're very proud of their history. You've seen the statues in Hero's Square? And see that.' He pointed across the rooftops to where the two ornate buildings Bond had been admiring stood proud. 'Their parliament and their big ugly church are both exactly the same height. Religion and government. Neither of them more important than the other. If I had my way, I'd bulldoze the whole bloody lot. History is boring. Only the future is important.'

'I hope you haven't had this conversation with your boss,' said Bond and Canner Lyle laughed darkly.

'My boss knows what kind of man I am, buddy,' he said. 'I'm a soldier. If you pay me, I will fight for you. I don't care who you are, or what you believe in. I think we understand each other, yes?'

'Two peas in a pod,' said Bond with a heavy dose of sarcasm.

He turned and smiled at the man. So familiar from the photographs in the file. Even wearing mirrored sunglasses that reflected Bond's own face back at him, he was easily recognisable.

Canner oozed vanity. This was someone who spent a lot of time in the gym, and wanted you to know it. He was wearing a light, tan military t-shirt with the sleeves rolled back to show as much of his bronzed, tattooed and knottily muscled arms as possible. No coat for Canner Lyle. Coats were for pussies. No doubt beneath his t-shirt was an immaculate, tight six-pack, ridged like a Toblerone.

He had the requisite shaved head and gleaming scalp of the hard man drowning in testosterone, and a closely shaved beard, so short it looked like it had been shaded in by a child with a pencil. The edges razored into lines so perfectly straight he must have used a metal ruler.

When he wasn't in the gym, he was probably to be found in a personal grooming salon. Bond wondered whether he applied the make-up that covered the flush of steroid acne on his lower face and neck himself. Or did he have it applied when he was getting pampered?

He had a slightly flattened nose and square jaw, as if he was permanently clenching his teeth, and fat veins stood out on his temples like slugs. There was a big, wireless ear bud sticking out of each ear, and the way he moved his head made Bond think that he was listening to music. Soundtracking his own life.

Headphone. Testosterone. Toblerone.

'So,' said Canner Lyle. 'My boss likes you. Feels he owes you a debt. When you rescued his wife in Croatia, you did yourself a good turn. Now I'm prepared to like you. But we have to go through some formalities first. Can I call you Pete?'

'No.'

'Ok. We'll play it your way. Shall we go somewhere more private to talk?'

'Whatever works for you, *buddy*.'

Lyle led Bond to one of the pods. As they walked, Bond was casually checking out the other guests, wondering how many of them were working for Lyle.

They went inside the white-framed igloo and settled into two sofas facing each other. There was an ice bucket on a table between them with six bottles of Dreher cooling in it. Lyle had obviously booked the igloo for their exclusive use. He took off his sunglasses, exposing his small eyes. He had very pale irises. As if all the colour had leeched out of them. It added an intensity to his stare.

'You don't seem very happy with me, my friend,' he said.

'Was it really necessary to put a tail on me, Lyle?' Bond asked.

'Please, call me Canner.' Lyle smiled. He fished a beer out of the ice bucket and popped the cap off with a key. He offered it to Bond who took it and sipped while Canner opened a second bottle. Once he was done, he saluted Bond with his beer and took a long pull.

Satisfied, he put the bottle down. 'We're thorough, my friend,' he said. 'Thorough and careful. You can understand that.'

'I can,' said Bond. 'Which is why I'm surprised it was so clumsily done. The Icelandic girl, Ragnheiður . . .' Bond studied Lyle's face as he spoke, checking for his reaction. The man kept things well under control, but there was a tell-tale bulge in one of his head-slugs. Bond was trained to spot these things. Did it without thinking. Gut sense.

'She's not bad,' he added. 'But I've seen better.'

'So, you've done your homework, my friend? Yes? Looked us up on Wikipedia? Maybe LinkedIn?'

He chuckled. They both knew that inside information about the Hauser Consultancy was extremely hard to find. Impossible without sophisticated hacking technology and a small army of tech-heads.

'I'm thorough,' said Bond, casually. 'Thorough and careful. I always like to know what I'm getting into.'

'Round one to you, I guess,' said Canner, slowly clapping his hands.

'I didn't know it was a competition.'

Lyle pointed his bottle at Bond and squinted. Smiling. Mano a mano. You and me, bud.

'We're men, my friend. Everything is a competition. There's nothing else in life that matters. Dog fucks dog, yeah? We understand these things.'

Bond smiled, tilted his own beer back at Canner. He didn't like the man, but had to stay in character. How different, really, though, was the character he was playing – a tough, cold, callous mercenary – to himself? A hired killer for the British government? They were both soldiers in their own way, and did Bond do what he did because of a sense of duty? Of service? For King and Country? Or was he as much a mercenary as this other man? Was there an element of self-loathing in his distaste for Canner? Were they actually the same, as Canner claimed? He'd been doing it for so long he didn't know any more.

'So.' Canner took another pull at his beer and then put it down purposefully. Ready to talk business. 'You obviously know something about us.'

'I know enough to have your boss put away if I wanted. Conspiracy, terrorism, recruitment of a private army . . .'

'Which is where you come in. What can you bring to the party?'

'As many guests as you need to make up the numbers.'

'I need specifics, my friend. We don't hire just any

45

old shooter off the street. Spell it out for me, how can you help our magnificent, criminal undertaking?'

'As much ordinance as you think necessary and 30 men. All ex-military. Mostly SAS. They all feel they've been let down one way or another by the powers that be. Always keen for payback.'

'Have you been let down too, Peter? Is that what brings you here?'

'I'm not stupid enough to do this for emotional reasons, Canner. Or ideological ones for that matter. You said yourself, we're both the same. All that concerns me is getting paid. If I sign on, it'll be for one thing, and one thing only – cold, hard cash.'

'Uh-uh.' Canner shook his bald head. 'Bitcoin, my friend. Untraceable. Easily transferable. The currency of the future.'

'Perhaps you weren't listening, Canner. I'll say it again. If I do this, it'll be for cold, hard cash. Not a string of code. Not a bank deposit. Cash money. You can put it in a wheelbarrow for all I care. But that's how I operate.'

'It's not how my boss operates, though. And this a deal breaker. Perhaps we can discuss this further?'

Bond put his bottle down on the table with an air of finality.

'You misunderstand the purpose of this meeting,' he said, standing up.

'I don't think I do,' said Lyle affably. 'It's a job inter-view.'

'Exactly,' said Bond, moving towards the exit. 'But

you're not interviewing *me*. *I'm* interviewing *you*. And you've failed. Have a nice day.'

Lyle laughed softly.

'No need for the theatricals, my friend. I've already vetted you. Or you wouldn't be here. But I wanted to meet you face to face. To see the whites of your eyes. You keep your light very surely hidden under a bushel. There's not a lot about you out there – which is impressive – and what we *could* find out we were even more impressed by. Stay and finish your beer at least.'

Bond hesitated. Then smiled and sat down. He had Canner where he wanted him. He'd taken one step closer to his prey.

April 11th – 25 days
until the Coronation

As the car emerged from a tunnel of dark pine trees, Bond got his first glimpse of the castle, squatting on top of one of the tree-covered hills that were so prominent here in the foothills of the Zemplén mountains that formed the border with Slovakia. The mountains where 009 had been taken. He must have still been alive, but only just. Probably bundled into the back of a window-less van. Driven to one of the popular climbing spots in the mountains in the dead of night. Taken up just high enough for his fall to look convincing and then dropped. Bond wondered whether Canner had been involved in that little excursion. Had he checked the fallen and broken body for any signs of life? Perhaps delivered the *coup de grâce* with a handy rock? As head of Æthelstan's security, he must at least have organised the killing, even if he himself hadn't carried it out. Bond had decided that whatever happened, and whatever the outcome of this mission, he would personally see to it that 'The Adventures of Canner Lyle' wouldn't make it to a second series.

He wondered, thinking back to his first Double O assignment and all that had happened since, exactly when he had begun to compartmentalise his feelings, and been able to think calmly and rationally about the act of killing. Just as a plumber might consider an upcoming job. The tools he'd need, the materials, how long it might take . . . Bond smiled and exhaled a soft snort of private laughter through his nose. He had no idea what plumbers did. Plumbing was a mystery to him. His was a strange peripatetic life. Living in hotels. Eating in restaurants. Plotting assassinations . . .

When had he first accepted that that was what he did? What he had to do.

At times like this, to keep the darkness at bay, he always told himself one thing. Killing people was what he did, not who he was. It was a small distinction, but he'd fought to keep that sentiment shut away in his heart, like a hard, precious jewel locked in a safe.

And this was stacking up to be one of the more deadly missions M had sent him on. Not least because time was short. There was no room for finesse, for careful plotting, for negotiation. He was a bullet and he'd already been fired from the gun. Nothing could stop him.

Except a brick wall. Or the jagged rocks at the foot of a cliff.

They were three hours out of Budapest, Bond sitting in the back of a black Land Rover Defender 130, being driven by Canner Lyle. Ragnheiður was next to him in the passenger seat, both of them taking turns to check him out in the rear-view mirror. Canner with a

49

piercing, slightly challenging look. Ragnheiður's elfin eyes unreadable.

He hoped they were both satisfied by what they saw. For his part he was trying to avoid eye contact by staring resolutely out of the window at the passing countryside.

There was one more passenger in the car. The bearded guy with the knitted cap from the tram. It turned out he was a Scotsman, Kenny Charlton. He seemed to be Canner's right-hand man and somehow managed to give off an air of geniality, good humour, rage and barely suppressed violence all at the same time. He'd no doubt been put back here with Bond to keep an eye on him. After what had happened with 009, Æthelstan and his organisation were going to be more suspicious than ever. And there was a certain smell of desperation. They were up against it. Not quite ready for their big day and clearly still hiring. Short of time; 009's intervention would have set them back. They'd probably doubled down on security since then. Bond wondered if 009 was the only one of their recruits they'd had to write out of the story.

The bottom line was that they evidently needed Bond's 30 men. And they needed Bond. Or Peter Sanbourne, as he now had to think of himself.

Canner's driving was fast and aggressive. He hung off the rear bumpers of drivers he deemed too slow, clearing the road with flashing lights and short blasts from the horn, cursing the other road users. All the while, he and Ragnheiður kept up a constant, low level, desultory bickering, like a long-time married couple, Ragnheiður only occasionally raising her voice to berate

Canner for a particularly unnecessary act of aggression. Most of the time she was disinterested, unfocused, but fidgety, fiddling with her phone, looking out of the window, changing radio stations on a whim. Jittery and restless. She had a cup of takeaway coffee that she kept going back to, each time appearing surprised that it was empty. Bond sneaked the occasional look at her. Drawn by her magnetic, vital air. Today she was dressed all in black – t-shirt, combat pants, heavy boots, and what looked like a Kevlar motorbike jacket.

Kenny kept up a non-stop stream of obscene jokes, obviously intended to annoy Ragnheiður. Crude and sexual. He'd just embarked on a long story involving some nuns, a priest and a vat of holy water.

It was hard to tell whether Ragnheiður had a sense of humour or not. The only person laughing was Kenny, in a peculiarly high-pitched, staccato way, whinnying like a demented horse.

They'd left the main road a while back and this was a remote, wild area. The castle must have been picked by Æthelstan for its relatively isolated location. As the road took a long, sweeping left curve, Bond could clearly see it now out of his window. According to the file, it had originally been built in the 17th century, but had been much altered and added to over the years, most recently during the Second World War, when it had been taken over by the military.

The main building, on top of the hill, had high, white walls, topped by steep gun-metal grey roofs. Built to shrug off the snow that would be heavy here in the winter. At the foot of the hill was a cluster of newer buildings that had the dull, depressingly functional look of army buildings. As far as the analysts at Vauxhall had been able to ascertain from their satellite surveillance, these buildings were being used as dormitories for Æthelstan's troops.

They turned off the road, passed through an ancient gateway manned by two bored-looking guards who opened the big iron gates just wide enough to let the Defender through, and waved them on their way.

They were now on a short, tree-lined driveway that headed towards the hill. Bond had already studied the castle from every angle back in Regent's Park. Even down to a floor plan from the war. What he was interested in now were the electricity lines that they'd been driving alongside for the last few kilometres, slung between recently erected pylons that marched across the fields and through the forests. The lines ran right up to the hill and connected to what the analysts assumed was a newly built substation, situated by the lower buildings and hidden from view by an overhang of rock.

Bond knew from the satellite images that the driveway would pass close by the presumed substation. He kept his gaze fixedly out of the window, and, sure enough, they soon came to a fenced-off area where the power lines angled down and linked up with a complex but orderly cluster of electrical equipment, with steel, lattice structures supporting strain bus wires and apparatus. He spotted several transformers, as well as high-voltage transformer fire barriers. Garish signs in English and Hungarian warned not to get too close.

DANGER: HIGH-POWER.

The question was *why*? Æthelstan had set himself up in an Anglo-Saxon fantasy castle, lit by candles and heated by fires. Why did he need to have a powerful electricity supply installed?

Was it to run machinery? Had he built a factory of some sort? Or was it needed for massive computing power and storage?

Whatever it was, it had nothing to do with Anglo-Saxon England.

Kenny was adding a lot of detail to his joke, stringing it out, doing cod Irish accents. '"And what about you, Sister Agnes, have you ever touched a man's private parts?" "Well now, Father, there was one time . . . just to see what it felt like, just the tip of my finger . . ." "Well then, dip your finger into the holy water and say three Hail Marys, Sister Agnes!"'

They left the substation behind and started up the hill, the driveway winding its way up, criss-crossing the slope. Eventually they arrived at a second set of gates. These ones were new and there was a little hut off to one side out of which came a guard. He looked considerably more on the ball than the two men at the outer gate. He walked up to the car, stiff-legged and self-important.

He was wearing a black, ballistic vest and cap and had a Heckler and Koch G36c semiautomatic carbine tightly slung across his chest, the barrel pointing at the ground. He was weighted down with extra gear, hanging from his nylon duty rig. A Glock 17 9mm sidearm, a telescopic baton, pepper spray, Speedcuffs, a 1TAC Tactical Flashlight, X25 taser and two TETRA radios.

Bond had been half-hoping that he would be going up against an eccentric, deluded Mickey Mouse outfit, trusting in God and St George to protect them, but these guys meant business. If the gatekeeper was so well-equipped, then Æthelstan's mercenary, shock troops were not going to be riding into battle with swords and spears.

The guard gave the car a once-over, exchanged eye-contact with Canner, and spoke briefly into one of his radios. He waited for a response and then nodded the car through.

They continued up the last bit of track to the front of the castle where there was a wide, open terrace with spectacular views across the landscape, which was a patchwork of green and yellow fields and dark, almost black, forests.

Uniformed staff emerged from the castle to pick up the bags from the back of the Defender and carry them inside. Bond hadn't known what to expect – whether the servants would be dressed like 7th century retainers in long, drab dresses, all pinnies and pigtails. But, in their smart, modern, forest green uniforms this could be an exclusive 5-star hotel.

The weather had turned. There was a light drizzle and a cold wind was whipping up the side of the hill. Canner and Ragnheiður led the small group inside, Kenny bringing up the rear, giggling at the punchline of his joke. Insisting on repeating it, in case any of them had missed it.

'"If I'm going to have to gargle with that stuff, Father

Michael, I want to do it before Sister Bridget sticks her arse in it."'

Just inside the doors was an airport-style security set up, with a metal detector and their suitcases already trundling along a conveyer belt that passed through an X-ray machine. Bond was glad he only carried what he needed to maintain his cover. There was nothing in his shell case or suit bag that would expose him as anything more than what he said he was. A gun for hire.

Especially as when his bags emerged at the other end of the machine, one of Æthelstan's female staff took them to one side, popped open the suitcase and started to rifle through it.

Bond watched as Canner removed his watch, phone, money, belt and keys and put them in a small plastic tray which he placed on the conveyor. When it came to his turn, Bond added his Glock 19 to the pile of items. It was a slightly more compact model of the sidearm that the guard at the gate carried. Glocks were pretty much standard issue for both private security and the military.

Canner raised an eyebrow at the sight of the gun. Bond merely shrugged and watched as the tray was swallowed by the ever-hungry mouth of the X-ray machine. He walked casually through the metal detector. He'd done this drill a thousand times; he could do it in his sleep, and he knew that nothing would set their lights flashing. It was just another dehumanising part of modern life.

Canner picked up his items and strolled off to make a phone call away from the others. Ragnheiður joined

Bond, who was patiently waiting for the girl to stop picking through his bag.

Ragnheiður tutted theatrically. 'Don't you mind a stranger exploring your most private space?'

'It's a suitcase,' said Bond. 'Not my inner soul.'

'I hope you don't have a typical Englishman's underwear.'

'I didn't know there was such a thing. What's wrong with an Englishman's underpants?'

'They are always old and baggy and have been washed too many times. Their wives buy them and their mothers.'

'Well, I have neither a wife nor a mother.'

'Poor, lonely boy.'

'Save your tears.'

'Tell me. Did you enjoy your little game of hide and seek in Budapest, Mister Peter Sanbourne?'

'Did *you*?'

'Hmm. I can't read you, Sanbourne. Is there anything going on beneath that attractive surface? Do you have depths, or is it all just dark, empty space?'

Bond shrugged. Said nothing.

'I have a theory that all good-looking men are stupid. Are you stupid, Mister Sanbourne?'

Bond shrugged again. 'I suppose it depends on what criteria you're using. I certainly wouldn't describe myself as an intellectual. If that's what you mean.'

'No Englishman ever does. Too shameful to admit.'

'I can count up to a hundred without using my fingers and I can calculate a twelve percent tip without using my phone, but I don't find Shakespeare's comedies funny. I only like poetry that rhymes, I don't get on with contemporary dance, even when they're semi-naked, and I've never read *Moby-Dick*.'

'Who has?'

'So, how did I score?'

'I'll let you know.'

'And what about women, Ragnheiður? Are all beautiful women stupid?'

'You tell me. You have the air of a man who's been around a few.'

'I lost count after a hundred,' said Bond with heavy irony. 'So, I guess that answers your question. My maths failed me. I must be stupid after all.'

Ragnheiður looked him up and down, coolly. 'Even stupid people have their uses . . .'

The girl had finally finished searching his bag. She'd neatly folded his clothes and closed the suitcase and now she smiled at Bond. All clear.

'I'll have it taken to your room, Mister Sanbourne. I have your ID badge here. You must wear it at all times.'

Bond went over to her. She passed him a plastic badge with his name and picture on it. It was attached to a lanyard, which he put round his neck.

'It will get you through all the doors and controls all the lifts to which you are allowed access.'

As she said this, she gave him back his tray of metal items. He'd expected the Glock to have been removed, but he immediately noticed that the phone was missing too. He looked over to where a security guard was putting the Glock and the phone into a numbered, plastic box. He then carefully wrote a number and a name onto a card with a Sharpie and slipped it into a slot on one end of the container. When he was done, he closed it and took it into a side room where there was a wall of cubby holes, each with one of the plastic boxes in it.

Someone slapped Bond on the back, and he turned to see Canner grinning at him, showing his canines.

'Making friends with Ragnheiður, I see, my friend. Be careful. She bites.' Canner snapped his teeth at Bond.

'Is it really necessary to take my phone?' said Bond. 'I still have business to do. I need to be able to communicate with my men.'

'Pretend it's the last century, buddy. People seemed to get by OK without cell phones. If you need to make a call there's a landline in the business suite. Along with a computer and printer, even a fax machine, if you can remember what one of them is. This really is the dark ages, hey? Just remember that everything is monitored. 24/7. Every moment you're in this castle there is someone watching you and someone listening to you. Hell, there's probably even someone smelling you! And if you smell off, my friend, they will see and hear you get hurt very badly. Now, go up to your room and take a shower. Dress for dinner. There's a reception at seven and dinner at eight.'

One of the staff showed Bond up the wide sweeping staircase to the first floor and then through a hidden side door that looked like part of the wall, to a smaller staircase which they climbed to the next floor. They walked down a long corridor with rooms on either side named after Saxon kingdoms – Mercia, Wessex, Northumbria, East Anglia. The girl stopped outside a door labelled 'Deira' and gestured for him to use his ID card. He pressed it against a flat black reader and the lock clicked open.

He thanked her, waited for her to leave and went in. He was gratified to find that his bags had been unpacked for him. His clothes neatly arranged between a wardrobe and a chest of drawers. The room was clean and warm and furnished with antiques. The bed a four poster.

The window looked out across fields and forest to the mountains. He gave the frame a quick once over. It was securely locked and glazed with laminated security glass. Very difficult to break. Was it to keep people out, or keep them in?

He took Canner's advice and stripped off. Not caring if he was being watched. A shower was a good place to think. He ran the water as hot as he could stand and adjusted the nozzle to deliver a hard, tight, pulsing jet. Nice to know that the castle's plumbing wasn't medieval.

As he let the water pound down onto his neck and shoulders, he turned the mission over in his mind. Where would 009 hide something? There was no point in being fiendishly clever and finding a hiding place where nobody would ever think of looking. Because one of those people might be a fellow agent. You have to know that if you fail, another agent would be infiltrated if at all possible. So it would have to be a hiding place that your fellow agent could discover by following a simple, logical process. That was the protocol. Hide in plain sight. Somewhere so obvious that nobody would look. Somewhere that was staring you in the face. No point in hammering away at the problem now. It was time for some gut sense. He let his unconscious mind take over. Let the primitive, non-rational, instinctive, animal brainstem communicate with his gut.

He turned his conscious thoughts to the girl, Ragnheiður. What had all that been about downstairs? Their little chat? The first one they'd properly had. What was the shape-shifting sea spirit up to? What magic was she weaving? He closed his eyes and luxuriated in the steaming water.

And saw her uptilted, elfin eyes staring back at him.

At five past seven, Bond was walking down the main staircase dressed for dinner. A hum of voices and music was coming from below. He was wearing a fitted dinner suit he'd had made for him by a tailor in Jaipur. A fraction of the price of Saville Row and almost as good quality. And there had been no questions asked about some of the modifications he'd asked for. His outfit was simple and understated. No fancy waist coat, an unfussy bow tie and black Oxfords. He wanted to blend in, not draw attention to himself. He was Peter Sanbourne. Someone who was serious about his job. He just hoped to God that everyone else wasn't going to be wearing cloaks and hoods and jingling about in chain mail. He'd reluctantly attended a cod medieval banquet once in Croydon. A young actress he was seeing was one of the 'cast members', which was a fancy term for a waitress, decked out as a comely wench with plunging neckline, serving beer in plastic drinking horns.

He never wanted to relive that experience.

One of Æthelstan's ever-helpful staff met him at the foot of the stairs and took him through to the reception. He was relieved to see that it was a low-key affair, with perhaps thirty people standing chatting in small groups. Music played discreetly from hidden speakers. Simple, repetitive piano music. The kind that students listened to while revising.

The room looked like the sort of bland function room you'd find in any smart, old hotel, with wood-panelled walls and a tiled floor. Staff were circulating with champagne and canapés. Bond grabbed an unidentifiable pastry thing and popped it in his mouth. Mushroom possibly. A little dry. He then took a full glass from a passing tray and washed down the last flakes of pastry with champagne. Not bad. A sensible Taittinger, nicely chilled. The thing about champagne was that once you went beyond a certain price, it didn't taste any better, and in many cases tasted worse.

He took another sip and scanned the room, trying to pick out any familiar faces from the file.

It didn't take him long to identify a handful.

For a coup to be effective you need representatives of the military, the media, the government, and the ordinary people. Æthelstan had done a pretty good job on that front. Even if most of the people in the room were only just this side of being certifiably insane. But then, insanity was the other characteristic you needed to buy into a cracked scheme like this.

Many of the men in the room could be described as 'ex' something – ex-military, ex-politician, ex-media pundit for hire. They'd become more and more extreme in their views and too toxic, unruly and unsafe to remain affiliated with the radical groups they'd joined. When you became too far out for a far-right organisation, you knew you were really on the outside.

But just look at them now, with their champagne and nibbles, their shiny shoes, their beaming faces. Almost to a man, dressed in uniform black tie. They were firmly on the inside and loving it. They'd found their tribe, and very soon they were going to announce themselves to the world. No longer outcasts, no longer cancelled, no longer marginalised, they were going to be the new overlords.

There was only one person standing between them and chaos.

James Bond.

In the middle of the room stood John Tyler, surrounded by a group of sycophants. Tyler was a good talker. A populist with the common touch. A hero to libertarians everywhere. A man 'brave enough to speak his mind'. He was an ex-football hooligan, ex-EDL member, who'd reinvented himself as a warrior fighting for truth and justice and had formed a pressure group called Knights of St George – champions of the ordinary men and women of England. Like many of the people in the room he'd been banned from social media and had his

YouTube channel taken down. You could still find him on there, of course, guesting on other people's shows, and he'd joined the online news channel 'The One Truth Network UK'. The channel had very murky backing and hosted a team of men and women like Tyler with a simplistic, dog whistle agenda of anti-Muslim, anti-immigrant, anti-Semitic, anti-EU, anti-North London Elite rhetoric. The plan was obvious, but effective – identify an enemy to bolster your own power base.

MI5 and MI6 had both had their eyes on Tyler for a long while as he simultaneously built an army of followers in England and made contacts with far-right groups in Europe, despite his anti-European stance.

He may have been banned from conventional social media, but he was all over the alternatives, sites like Gab, Telegram, Rumble and Truth Social. And there was a meme of him that was still doing the rounds on Twitter. John Tyler on the beach at Dover saying earnestly into a camera, 'England for the English – I'm sorry, but how is that controversial?'

Tyler was talking to a man in pink trousers and a blue blazer. The only splash of colour among the sea of black and white. The trousers belonged to the eccentric aristocrat, Lord Anthony Saxewell-Brooks. A knack for deliberately controversial pronouncements and a string of illegitimate children had earned him the tabloid nickname, 'Lord Bonkers'. His family had owned a castle and a vast tract of land in the west country since time immemorial. He was famous for trying to promote a return to Victorian values, despite cheating on his wife with their nanny, marrying the nanny, and then cheating on her with the new nanny, while simultaneously carrying on an affair with his neighbour's wife. He was a physically unprepossessing man, but vast wealth evidently made him irresistible. About five years ago he'd shot at a group of activist trespassers with a twelve-gauge shotgun. A team of expensive lawyers had got all charges dropped. He'd been a major donor for the Conservative party before announcing that they were too far to the left. He was now one of the backers of a libertarian group called the 'New Freedom Party'.

John Tyler and Lord Bonkers were laughing loudly. The British working classes had more in common with, and shared more of the views of, the upper classes than either of them did with the middle classes. Especially the hated metropolitan elite.

Speaking of the 'New Freedom Party', its leader, Roger Birkett, was chatting with another group of men next to John Tyler's group. They were more serious. There was a lot of head nodding going on. They were the grown-ups at the party. The sweaty red of their faces accentuated by their monochrome dinner suits.

Birkett was an ex-Tory MP, famous for promoting covid/vaccines/mask-wearing/5G conspiracy theories, which had spilled over into the usual anti-immigrant, anti-EU, anti-BBC, anti-MSM, anti-cultural Marxist, Climate Change Denial pronouncements. It was an anti-trans diatribe that had eventually got him kicked out of the party and he'd soon after set up the 'New Freedom Party'.

Bond was struck by something. It was a long while since he'd been at any kind of function that was almost exclusively full of men. It felt strange. There was not even a pretence at diversity here. Æthelstan hadn't been the least bit concerned about ensuring that half of the people he'd hired to carry out his coup should be women, or non-white, or disabled. This was an unapologetically old-school gathering. In Æthelstan's world he was king and could do whatever he wanted. That was the whole point, and it was why his followers loved him. These men had bought into his fantasy, and many of them had supplied him with shock troops, who were down in the compound at the foot of the hill. The men that Bond had promised Canner should have all joined them by now. There was a lot of sweaty male energy in this room, a lot of testosterone flying around. Bond couldn't imagine what it must be like down in the camp.

As he looked around, he recognised more and more of the men – two members of the German Reichsbürger Patriotic Union, talking to Kaspar Faust, a German neo-Nazi, and Lawrence Lancaster, co-founder of The Knights of St George with John Tyler. He was apparently the money and the brains behind the outfit. All three of them were dressed in black tie. No jackboots or flak jackets in this crowd. They were civilised people.

And over there was Captain Perry Hughes, talking to Canner Lyle and Kenny Charlton. On leaving the army, Hughes had gone into mainstream politics. Standing as an independent, focused entirely on single issue politics – namely 'No Wind Farms In Our Beautiful

Unspoilt Part of England.' He failed to get elected but the media loved him. He was passionate, good-looking and clean-cut. He'd featured in a couple of reality programmes and had been lined up to present his own series until he was filmed in a pub on someone's phone giving a drunken rant about Jews running the media before breaking someone's jaw in the subsequent fight.

On emerging from prison he'd disappeared, and Bond was intrigued to find him here in this company.

But where was Æthelstan? Was he not going to come to his own party? Or was he waiting to make a dramatic entrance?

Bond circulated among them. Working the room. Picking up scraps of information and gossip. It wasn't his job to fight culture wars, but when they threatened to spill over into a real war, then that was different.

The men he talked to invariably started with what shows they'd been streaming, sport, travel, women, cars, and soon moved on to laughing about how much they hated cyclists and bus lanes and congestion charging, and traffic calming, and how global warming was a con, and sooner or later came round to the Big Woke Conspiracy, Black Lives Matter, the Great Replacement, and what are we going to do about the Muslims?

Bond was taking a breather and getting a refill, when a big Frenchman joined him. He was getting a top up himself, although his glass was over half-full.

'So, you are Peter Sanbourne? *Oui*?'

'That's me. And I know who you are – Renaud Caiboche. Something of a role model for me.'

This was indeed Renaud Caiboche. Ex-French Foreign Legion. Now the main man behind a private mercenary organisation. He'd recruited many disgruntled and rootless ex-service men and women and his organisation specialised in helping autocratic governments, mainly in Africa and the Middle East, defeat rebel forces.

Recently Caiboche had shown some political ambitions. Trying to gain support, unsuccessfully, in the French elections. He had a neck so thick it looked wider than his great square head, which was covered in wiry, grey stubble. All this on top of the massive, powerful body of a French rugby player.

'But you are stepping on my feet, Sanbourne,' he said. 'Coming into my back yard. My territory.' The man's manner was polite, but with an unmistakable hint of menace. 'I've checked out your resumé. Very impressive. But how is it I've never come across you before? When we operate in the same area.'

'I don't know, Caiboche,' said Bond, matching Caiboche's polite tone, but with a hard edge of his own. 'Perhaps it's because I'm more discreet than you. I'm not in the business of self-promotion. I keep my head down and get on with things. My operations are almost exclusively undercover.'

'Even so . . .'

Bond had spotted Æthelstan's wife, Marina. So far, the only female presence in the room. She caught his eye and smiled warmly.

Bond nodded to Caiboche, cutting him off. 'Will you excuse me?'

67

There was a flicker of irritation across the Frenchman's face.

'Of course.'

As he went over to join Marina, Bond felt a slight pang of guilt about the trick he'd pulled on her. Staging the hijack and his gallant rescue. But at least she had an exciting story to tell her friends as they had their nails done, or drank cocktails at sunset on Æthelstan's yacht.

'Mister Sanbourne. How lovely to see you again.' She had only a faint trace of her Swiss accent. 'I can't tell you how pleased I am you've joined my husband's undertaking.'

'The feeling's mutual,' said Bond. 'This is a hell of a gathering. It's an amazing opportunity to be part of something like this.'

Marina turned to the man next to her, a celebrity British criminal with a reputation for extreme violence, who'd slipped off the radar.

'Mister Sanbourne was kind enough to save me from a very dangerous situation,' she explained to him.

'That so?' The thug tipped his glass towards Bond. He looked slightly dubious.

And he had a right to be. It hadn't been a dangerous situation at all. It had all been meticulously planned.

Bond had trained for three days with Dan, Yuri and Ben, the lads from Special Operations. Tough as nails. Ex-marines. Did the day-to-day dirty work for MI6. The grunt work. The fight had been meticulously choreographed, right down to the optimal speed that Bond should clip Ben's bike at. The punches and kicks had been designed to look far worse than they actually were, and the lads were protected by padded Armortec jackets, elbow pads, knee pads and the latest D30 stunt armour vests, which stay flexible until impact and then instantly harden.

They'd carefully picked the ideal place to stage the fight, so that they'd have enough space and wouldn't kill Carl when they chucked him over the crash barrier.

Not only had this little charade got Bond close to Æthelstan, they'd also been able to extract a mine of useful information from Marina's phone.

Tonight she was wearing a black and silver dress with jewellery that was designed to look flashy and expensive. Bond knew from her file that she was 45, but you'd be hard pressed to work out her age just from seeing her in the flesh and would guess at early thirties. A lot of money, a lot of pampering, some skilled, light surgery, a tailored diet and a lack of stress had kept her young-looking.

'This is all so . . . thrilling,' she said. 'But also . . . *terrifying*. Such a risk.'

'A risk worth taking.'

'Cheers to that,' said the thug and he drained his glass before wandering off to get a top up.

'I hope so,' said Marina. 'I certainly hope so.'

Bond was reminded of the fact that behind every aspiring despot was a woman worried about her husband and family.

'Don't worry,' said Bond. 'He's got the best men for the job.'

Marina smiled distantly and looked away, as if her mind was elsewhere, still focused on the risk. Was she wondering if all this was going to be taken away from her? Then she saw something, and her look turned sour.

Bond followed her gaze.

Marina was no longer the only female in the room.

Ragnheiður had joined them, wearing a statement white dress made of scrunched tissue-thin layers. Like a bride arriving at her wedding reception. She was younger than Marina; more alive. She turned heads.

Bond checked his watch. It was nearly eight. Ragnheiður hadn't been in any hurry to get here. He was more used to seeing her dressed to kill – in the literal sense. He'd not seen her 'dressed to kill' in the fashion sense before. She really was a shape shifter. Appearing in whatever form took her fancy at any time.

She moved among the men like a spirit. Aloof. Unsmiling. She got herself a drink and approached Marina and Bond. She barely nodded hello to Marina and then looked Bond up and down with a slightly dismissive look.

'Another black and white sheep following the flock. I've always found something . . .' she shuddered in mock disgust as she searched for the right word. '*Threatening* about a room full of men in dinner suits. Like an army of clones. Ugly. At least yours fits you – not like some of the men here.'

She looked around the room with disdain.

'I love your dress,' said Marina, making conversation. 'Where's it from?'

Ragnheiður shrugged. 'A shop.'

There was an awkward pause. The three of them standing there, not knowing what to say.

They were saved by the music changing and the lights dimming. The polite, bland piano music had been replaced by something bombastic and classical that Bond didn't recognise. There was a great sense of anticipation amongst the guests and a hushed murmur passed between them as the wood panels down one wall began to fold back automatically. It was a moment of theatre, like a curtain parting to reveal . . .

To reveal what looked very much like a stage set. Albeit on a massive scale. It was a monumental banqueting hall, rising the full height of the castle, some three storeys, with rough stone walls, flagstones and rushes on the floor. Three monstrous iron chandeliers blazing with candlelight hung down from a complex wood-beamed ceiling, like the inside of an upturned boat.

Everything here was done a massive scale. Logs were burning in a fireplace that, if it was in London, could be rented out as a bijou flat. And down the centre of the hall was an oak table that must have been made from half a forest. There were benches ranged along each side of the table, apart from where there was a row of high-backed chairs – the central one higher than the others and with more elaborate carving. It looked like a throne.

On the wall behind the throne hung a tapestry, depicting a Saxon king being crowned. The king was clearly Æthelstan himself. Above the tapestry was a big coat of arms.

Bond had studied heraldry for a case he'd been assigned to a few years ago, and he knew enough to know that coats of arms were an invention of the Middle Ages. King Alfred the Great, and his grandson, Æthelstan, wouldn't have had their own arms back in the day. So medieval heralds had retro-fitted one for the Kings of Wessex. These arms, representing the late Anglo-Saxon kings, especially Edward the Confessor, had first appeared in a manuscript in the 13th century – blazoned as Azure, a cross patonce between five martlets which, in layman's terms, meant a gold cross with arms of the same length on a blue background with golden birds in the spaces between them.

A spontaneous round of applause broke out and everyone started talking loudly as the servants ushered them into the hall. There was a seating plan on a stand, with the names hand-written in cursive script. Bond soon found his place at the table, on a bench directly opposite the throne, between Caiboche and Roger Birkett.

Once they were all seated, the wall slid back into place and the illusion that they'd travelled back in time was complete.

Bond had only been inside a Disney theme park once. In Paris. When a contact had insisted on meeting him there, claiming it was one of the safest and most secure places in Europe. No chance of any ambush there.

Bond had been impressed by the skill and artistry that had gone into its design and construction. It was a totally immersive fantasy world, with its three-quarter scale streets and castles, its waterways and rides, the fake taverns, the fake rocks and forts, but he'd found the overall effect slightly second-hand and cloying.

Stepping inside this banqueting hall had a similar effect on him. It was ersatz. Inspired by cinema more than real life. And what a bizarre mash up of different times and cultures it was. The backdated coat of arms was the perfect illustration of how phoney this set up was. Here they were in a 17th century Hungarian castle, fitted out like a 12th century English banqueting hall, trying to conjure up the life of a Saxon king who'd lived some 200 years previously in a time when there were no castles in England, only wooden hill forts and earls' halls.

The noise level had risen noticeably in here, echoing off the cavernous walls. The sense of anticipation had risen as well. The throne was still empty. But it was ready, so Æthelstan must be arriving soon. The seats on either side of it had been taken by Marina and Ragnheiður, and the other two high-backed chairs were filled by Canner Lyle and Kenny Charlton. Bond watched as Canner picked up a loaf from a platter and tore off a chunk as if he was tearing the head off an enemy.

Now a fanfare blasted from the speakers and spot-lights picked out a raised platform at one end of the hall, on which stood a lectern with two thin, stick microphones fixed to it. As the last notes of the fanfare died away, four immense Irish wolfhounds stalked onto the platform through a pair of big oak doors and stood obediently at the front, staring at the guests.

A moment later, Æthelstan appeared through the doors and the place erupted. The men standing up from their seats and cheering, whistling, roaring and clapping.

Bond had to admit, it was quite an entrance. This whole show was expertly stage-managed. Whatever else he was, Æthelstan was certainly a polished huckster.

There he stood in all his Saxon glory, his long hair brushed back from his face, his moustache bristling. No staid dinner suit for him. He was draped in heavily embroidered robes, blue and red and gold, and somehow, the effect was not entirely ludicrous. The man had the balls to pull it off. He was even wearing the gold circlet around his head that he'd been wearing in the photograph that Bond had first been shown by M.

Since then, Bond had studied dozens of other photographs – Æthelstan, clean-shaven in his City days wearing a range of power-business suits, Æthelstan in black tie at various swanky functions, Æthelstan in flak jacket and flying helmet, Æthelstan in full country shooting garb holding up a brace of dead pheasants.

One thing Bond had learned in reading about the man was that, amazingly, he had actually been christened Æthelstan, by an eccentric father who had been as obsessed by Anglo-Saxon Britain as his son, but whose surname was the more mundane Wells.

Æthelstan acknowledged the applause with a wide-mouthed grin and looked over his gathered guests with his bulging eyes. Delighted. Now he fished out a pint of beer in a dimpled glass tankard from behind the lectern and raised it in a toast.

'What a shower!' he said, once the noise had died down, eliciting a fresh wave of laughter. 'Who let you lot in? Ha-ha-ha-ha-ha.'

He had the hale and hearty voice of a Kentish yeoman. Rich and slightly drawling. He could be the landlord of the Black Bull in Maidstone, raising a pint pot of good old English ale to his regulars from his station at the optics.

'Seriously, though,' he went on. 'You lot, you guys, are the bloody best.' A cheer. 'The backbone of England. Even though half of you aren't English at all – ha-ha-ha-ha-ha. But you know what I mean. Wherever you're from, you understand that a country – any country – if it's worth its salt, must stand for something. Many people think I'm utterly old-fashioned and out of touch, but do you know what? I couldn't care less. I believe in the idea of nationhood. A country must *mean* something. Or what is it? Just a place full of random people. A meaningless blob of diverse men and women. Oh, sorry, not allowed to call them that anymore, are we?'

Hoots of laughter. Catcalls.

'But you lot. You haven't been bamboozled and brain-washed by all this trendy, leftist tommyrot. And you're prepared to stand up for your principles. You're prepared to do something. To *be* something. To stand and fight. You are the 300 Spartans at Thermopylae, ready to lay your lives on the line to keep the hated foreign invaders out. You are the boys in red at Rorke's Drift, holding back an army of Zulus. You are the Paras taking on the Argentines at Goose Green . . .'

Some cries of 'Yes!'

'But you also understand one crucial thing. The greatest enemy is not a foreign invader, it's not a Persian, or a Zulu, or an Argie, it's the enemy among us. The greatest threat comes from those who try to undermine our great country from within. Be it a biased BBC journalist with a hidden agenda, a beardie from Islington who thinks we should all ride vegan bicycles and worship at the altar of Karl Marx, or a man in a dress who insists we call him "they".

'And – listen – no, listen, stop your laughing – this is serious – it can even be a member of our own so-called "Royal Family". So, gentlemen . . .' He looked over and picked out Ragnheiður and Marina. 'And *ladies. Real* ladies!'

A smattering of laughter. Bond caught Ragnheiður's eye. She looked amused. But it was inner amusement, as if at a private joke.

'I'm going to speak to you in plain English. The greatest language in the world. Because you deserve that respect.' Æthelstan was sounding more serious now. 'I'm not going to dress up what I say in flim-flam and gobbledegook. England has been betrayed. And I'm here to ask you tonight, gentlemen, and ladies, what we are going to do about it?'

He paused for a moment to look around the hall before continuing. 'On May the sixth, Charles Windsor, or, more properly, Charles Saxe-Coburg-Gotha, is going to be officially crowned King at Westminster Abbey, by the Archbishop of Canterbury, in a ceremony going back a thousand years. But he won't be crowned King of England. No. Because we don't have such an entity. He will be crowned King of the United Kingdom of Great Britain and Northern Ireland. What an ugly mouthful that is. Sounds like it was put together by a committee. What we need is a proper King of England. Not this watered-down imitation. This "Chairperson of the UK". I'll tell you the only good thing about this coronation – the pubs will remain open for an extra two hours!'

A big cheer.

'They've taken our history, our culture, our great legacy, and tossed it in the bin. Turned it all into a pantomime, a charade. King Charles III? Perhaps we should better call him "King Charles the Woke". His great-grandfather, George V, ruled an Empire of over 400 million people that covered nearly 14 million square miles. Nearly a quarter of the world's population and a quarter of the earth's total land.

'And what happened to it all? What did they do with it? They gave it away. Because it wasn't *nice* to have an Empire.

'Elizabeth sat on that throne for 70 years. Our longest reigning monarch. Like everyone else, I loved that woman. Loved and admired her. But I hated the fact that she wasn't allowed to actually do anything, to actually rule. She was applauded for keeping her head down and her mouth shut. But is that really all we want from our monarchy? To not make a fuss? I'm ashamed of what has become of my country. I am English. I can trace my line directly back to my namesake, Æthelstan, and from there to his grandfather, Alfred the Great. The GREAT!'

He pointed over to where the tapestry was rising up the wall to reveal a big white screen, on which was projected an image of Æthelstan's supposed family tree, with a big, stylised, white dragon at the top of it. To anyone not trained in genealogy it looked impressive. But Bond knew that there were some pretty imaginative leaps in it.

'See!' Æthelstan shouted. 'Some great names on there. Edmund Ironside. Æthelflæd, Lady of the Mercians, Edward the Confessor . . . And greatest of all, Alfred himself. Alfred the Great. Born in the year 848. He created England, and his daughter preserved it. Æthelflæd, one of the greatest women in history. A warrior. A leader. Even with her father dead she was able to keep his dreams alive. She would have eaten Charlie-boy for breakfast. And she will! Because these people here, these Anglo-Saxons – they are the true English!

'Look at this family tree. One thing should be abundantly clear to you – that Charles does not legitimately have the right to inherit the throne. No right at all! I have a more direct lineage back to the true English kings – Alfred, Æthelstan, Edgar, Edmund, Edward the Confessor.'

Bond poured himself another glass of wine and tried not to show his disdain for Aethelstan's speech. It was spurious to say the least. There was no acknowledgement that the English were outsiders, invaders, themselves. They were Germanic tribesmen, Angles and Saxons and Jutes, who'd displaced the indigenous Celtic Britons, driving them into

Wales and Cornwall and Scotland. Why pick one small point in history? Why not try to put a Celt on the throne? Or go further back and put a Neanderthal there?

It seemed there was no stopping Æthelstan, though. He was waving a hand in the air, now, as he ranted on.

'Charles Saxe-Coburg-Gotha is not English, Elizabeth was not English, Queen Victoria was not English, none of the damned bloody lot of them were English. After William the Bastard invaded, our monarchs were Norman, French, Dutch and now German. Anything but English. There is no purity of blood. Only a true born Englishman with a heart of British oak can make England English again.'

That brought a rousing cheer, and Æthelstan rode it, his speaker system powerful enough to make him heard over the din.

'The problems all started with William the Conqueror bringing the bloody frogs over to England. The frogs who have lorded it over us ordinary English for a thousand years. They call themselves the elite! A French word, of course. *Elite* . . .'

Boos and catcalls. A shout of 'Rule Britannia'.

'Since that time, the English have never been allowed to be what they are, to be English. Our country is no longer even a sovereign state. Our land became rebranded as Great Britain, and then the United Kingdom, and England got forgotten in the process. And now English voices are ignored. England is the power house of the United Kingdom, it's where the wealth is made, where the manufacturing centres are, where the food is grown. But are we allowed to say these things? No! We need to properly take back control! Take back England. Leaving the bloody European Union was only the first step. The next is to leave the United Kingdom, to break it up and return England's stolen glory. We can do it, you and I! I have the plans, I have the money, I have the manpower, I have the media.

'We will disrupt, we will make a noise, we will create an event and we will broadcast our message! The English are coming! We will show the world just what we're capable of. Because they don't know. They have misjudged us. Let me ask you how the English are seen abroad, in America, Europe and the Far East.

'I'll tell you,' he said. 'They see the English as limp-wristed fops, sarcastic, snooty and supercilious. Witty gents like Hugh Grant, David Niven, Noel Coward, Benedict Cumberbatch and Eddie Redmayne – Alan Rickman as the Sheriff of Nottingham! Lily-livered and pale. Englishmen never take their shirts off in Hollywood movies, but they do know how to wear a nicely tailored Savile row suit. They're posh boys with stiff upper lips, but limp everywhere else. The thing is, though, these aren't Englishmen. No! They're not Saxons, they're Normans! They're bloody French! The hated elite who've undermined our country for hundreds of years, like leeches sucking at us. Living off the backs of stout Saxon men.' He laughed and looked along the table at Caiboche. 'Apologies to my French friend.'

'No need to apologise,' said Caiboche with a smile. 'The true French. The Franks. We are descended from

Germans, too. Just like you English. I have no love for Macron's France.'

Bond glanced round at Caiboche – too far right for Le Pen. What *did* the Frenchman love? Violence and mayhem by the look of him. No other reason for him to have signed on to this Saxon fest.

'I'll ask you another question,' said Æthelstan. 'When are we ever allowed to identify ourselves as coming from "England"? I'll tell you when – at international football matches. At the World Cup. And what happens when our English lads try to show their pride and support – they're branded hooligans.'

Shouts of 'Shame!' A small group started singing, 'Three Lions On Your Shirt'.

'The elite!' Æthelstan yelled, almost screaming. 'The smug, French, liberals in their huge mansions. They put down our hooligans. They attack them and belittle them and sneer at them. Saying this is not the image of England we want to present to the world. But our brave boys, supporting our national team, they are the true English. They keep the Anglo-Saxon spirit alive. They're the true patriots.'

Bond could see John Tyler nodding and grinning, shouting his support.

Æthelstan waited for silence and then carried on. 'Wasn't it Cecil Rhodes who said "Ask any man what nationality he would prefer to be, and ninety-nine out of a hundred will tell you that they would prefer to be Englishmen"?'

That went down well. Although Caiboche didn't smile.

'And somebody in this room once said, "England for the English – how is that controversial?"' The shouts from the room threatened to drown out Æthelstan now, so he raised his voice even higher. 'And, by God, they were right! Being called English is like being called a paedophile. The great Winston Churchill once said "There is a forgotten, nay almost forbidden word, which means more to me than any other. That word is England." Yes! England. Home of the white dragon. I'm English, and I'm proud of it. So, I'll say it now! England for the English.'

The room erupted and Æthelstan shouted over the top of the cheering:

'Whet the bright steel, Sons of the White Dragon!
'Kindle the torch, Daughter of Hengist!'

Once the cheering had died down, Æthelstan ploughed on, waving his blood-stained banner, but Bond tuned him out. He'd heard enough. Until the old windbag got onto something concrete about what he intended to do, Bond wasn't interested. Frankly, he was confused. He had no emotional investment in the speech and so was able to sit back and break down what Æthelstan was saying without getting swept up in the rhetoric. Each line, taken in isolation, hit home and made some kind of sense, but put together they didn't add up to a coherent argument. Æthelstan was firing off wildly at all kinds of targets, making a lot of noise, but the speech was rambling and unfocused. It lacked any kind of logic. Some of it was about the loss of Empire and influence, but that had nothing to do with Anglo-Saxon

Britain. It was a British empire, not an English one. The speech was an all-purpose, jingoistic mishmash.

A classic magician's sleight of hand. Dazzle your audience, give them what they want, make them see what you want them to see, and distract them from the trick you're pulling on them.

The Internet was drowning in this kind of hogwash. And the likes of MI5 and MI6 were constantly having to monitor it, trying to spot anyone who was getting too radicalised and might start collecting semi-automatic weapons and making bombs. It starts with a disaffected young man. He feels powerless and unloved and wants someone to blame. He goes searching online and comes across an equally sad and lonely ally, realises that they feel EXACTLY what he does. They're just as confused and angry and scared. He reaches out to them. Befriends them. Now he's not alone. And soon they're joined by others. Suddenly it's a movement and they realise that EVERYONE feels this way. That they're right to think the way they do. They've inflated their bubble and they feel safe inside it. All sense of perspective, of objectivity, has long gone. Everybody feels like they do.

Except for those that don't. They can't deny that there are others out there who think differently. And who are they? They must be the enemy. They're organised and they're trying to stop you from telling the truth. So now you have to take action. You have to make a statement. Tear something down. Kill someone. Blow something up. Hit back at *them*.

Whoever *they* are.

Æthelstan's private army was a toxic mix. Some were losers looking for validation. Others were thugs who enjoyed violence and wanted justification for it. They were the descendants of all those crusaders pouring out of the west into the Holy lands. Disgruntled ex-military. Professional private security firms looking to make a hit. But just what the hell was Æthelstan's plan? Bond wished he'd get round to it. He could send these zealots into battle, and some would fare better than others, some would survive longer. Most were cannon fodder. But cannon fodder served a purpose. They soaked up enemy fire while you got your big guns into position. What were Æthelstan's big guns? What ammunition was he using? Bond returned his attention to the man in the gold circlet. It looked like he might finally be getting to the point.

'I'm not going to bullshit you. It's not going to be easy. We'll have to go in hard. Like a commando force. And when I say we're going commando, I don't mean we won't be wearing any underpants! We will be using guerrilla tactics, SAS tactics, special forces tactics. One man can make a difference. A hundred men can make a big difference. Five hundred men can change the world. Small, well-trained units, hitting key points, can cause enormous disruption. There are a handful of traffic pinch points around London. Block them and you bring central London to a standstill. At the same time, we'll shut down the power grid, we'll cause a computer blackout, we'll get into parliament, make the Capitol riots look like Aunt Fanny's tea party. We can do these things, and we *will* do all these things. We'll get into the BBC, with its pathetic security system, its guards outsourced to some godforsaken outfit like Rentokil, and once we've shut down the hated Mainstream Media, we will shut down Buckingham Palace, Parliament! You, each of you, with your own units know what to do. We will create maximum havoc. We will ensure that Charles is not crowned on the 6th.'

A big cheer for that one.

'But it'll all kick off on the 4th. That's the big day. Do you know what's so significant about May 4th?'

The room fell quiet apart from some dull murmuring. The guests shook their heads, looked to each other.

'I'll tell you – it's my birthday! And this year, as a birthday treat, my new news channel will be going live. Consolidating all of your various networks into one blockbuster channel. Originating here, but broadcasting from outer space. Not under the jurisdiction of any government, any earthbound organisations. They won't be able to shut us down. We will be free to speak the truth! And on the 4th the truth will be out there. So that our people will be ready and waiting for the final revelations on Coronation Day – when we will be *really* making the news!

'"Cry havoc and let slip the dogs of war!"'

People were on their feet now, stamping and cheering.

'We will spread chaos, confusion, disorder, devastation, turmoil, turbulence, lawlessness . . . We will create Armageddon. And out of that ruin will rise a new monarchy. You want to know why? Because the English people are crying out for it. The people will rise and join us. Once we shine a light on the lies they're fed and show them the real truth. Charles will not take the throne. The coronation will not happen. And the English will take back their country.

'We will create a spark that will light a fuse, that will detonate an explosion and our names will be written in flames across the heavens. Our names will ring down the years. We will be celebrated by bards and balladeers, by YouTubers and TikTockers. This will mark the end of a travesty. The end of the ordinary Saxons kowtowing to the French elite. The end of history. And the return of the English.

'WE ENGLISH!'

He stopped and looked at the people seated at the table. Taking in their eager faces and making eye contact – one by one. A hush descended. Finally, he raised both hands above his head.

'I am the king in waiting. I'm King Arthur ready to return to England in its hour of greatest need. I am the future!'

The spotlight cut out, plunging Æthelstan into darkness. The crowd bayed.

Bond was clapping along. Keeping up the pretence. But he had one thought in his mind.

Not if I can help it.

It was hot in his room and Bond could find no way of adjusting the heating, so he lay, naked, on his big four poster bed, replaying Æthelstan's speech in his head.

What was the man up to? He must know that his attack would end in bloody failure. There had to be something else going on. Were there any clues in what he'd said? Had 009 got deep enough to find out? And, if so, where had he hidden the evidence?

Bond went over the events of the evening again.

After the speech, Æthelstan had joined them at the table, acting the genial host as platter after platter of food was brought in and set before them. It was a meat-heavy feast, beef and lamb and pork, broken up by elaborate sea food platters, bristling with claws and shells, giant fat prawns, lobsters, langoustine, oysters, crayfish and mussels.

Æthelstan had only one rule for the feast: 'No talking shop. No business, and nothing about Operation 848. Understood? I want to enjoy my grub, thank you very much.'

He'd cracked jokes, fired off anecdotes, asked questions, making sure to include everyone around him. He was a professional entertainer.

Along with the food came jugs of beer and wine. And it was drinkable stuff too. Æthelstan had a pretty good cellar. He hadn't used the jugs to disguise inferior quality wine.

Before the dessert course a photographer set up a small stepladder at one end of the table and they all had to pose for the inevitable group photograph. Raising a glass – *cheers!* – to the camera.

'Come on, you lot!' Æthelstan goaded them. 'You pay for your pleasures!'

Bond had made sure to keep his face partly turned away and obscured by a full wine glass. He'd found the whole thing awkward, bathetic and macabre. Like one of those videos on YouTube – 'Last pictures taken of people before they died.'

Before they'd finished their dessert, things had got out of hand. Caiboche had been telling Æthelstan how much he'd enjoyed the speech.

'And I have to agree,' he'd said. 'The English are not what they once were. I pity you. You once were a nation of fighters. You love to fight. But now you are not good at it. Or why would you be hiring a Frenchman like me to help you?'

John Tyler, a few seats away, had been listening to their conversation.

'Oi!' he shouted down the table at Caiboche. 'Enough of that. Æthelstan hasn't only hired frogs. You're the minority here, Jonjo.'

'*Non*,' said Caiboche. 'Æthelstan has hired some English hooligans, too. But the days of English hooligans being feared is over. All I see now is boys fighting on beaches in flipflops. In Russia, the hooligans train. Putin is proud of his hooligans. They show the true spirt of Russian men, hard and dangerous. But, even so, in France we have the best.'

'What a lot of bollocks,' said John Tyler angrily. 'The English taught the world how to commit violence at football.'

'The English taught the world a lot of things, John Tyler, but sadly they didn't learn those lessons themselves.

England has become decrepit, degenerate, moribund, dissolute. Soft and weak.'

'Not the true English. We still have hearts of oak.'

'Heads of oak, perhaps. The French have always beaten the English. Even a little French girl beat the English. Jeanne D'Arc.'

'We slaughtered you at Waterloo!' John shouted. 'We are fighters. Always were. Always will be. Under the cross of St. George, the warrior saint. We never surrendered to Hitler.'

'Oh, it always comes to this.'

'Yes, it does. You want to prove how tough you are? You want to fight?'

So saying, Tyler climbed up onto the table, kicking dishes and platters out of the way, knocking over glasses. He swayed slightly. Evidently, he'd enjoyed one jug too many of Æthelstan's ale.

'Do I want to fight?' Caiboche laughed. 'No. I do not. This is not the place to fight.'

'Why not? Why can't this be the place? Eh?'

'It would be disrespectful.'

'I'll fight any man here,' John said. 'Prove to you what I am. What the English are. I'll take on anyone at this table. Come on. Let's do it.'

Bond looked over at Æthelstan, wondering how he was going to deal with this. How he was going to maintain his authority. Æthelstan was whispering something into Canner's ear. Canner nodded. Stood up.

'You want a fight, John Tyler?' he said, jumping onto the table from a standing start. 'I'll give you a fight.'

John Tyler let his breath out in a long sigh. Bond saw a flash of fear pass through his eyes and they flicked about uncertainly.

'Lyle,' he said. 'This isn't your fight.'

'What's the matter, John, you scared?'

'Course I ain't fucking scared.' John puffed out his chest and jutted his chin forward.

The other guests started rhythmically slapping their hands on the table. One or two started to chant 'fight-fight-fight-fight'. The others joined and hand slaps became fists, drumming louder and harder.

'Alright, then,' said John. 'Let's get on with it.' He charged down the table.

Just before he got to Canner, Kenny slid a silver platter towards him, catching him between the legs. John's feet went back from under him and, as he stumbled forward, Canner caught him under the chin with his foot, flipping him over. John landed with a crash on the table and a great cheer went up from the men, mixed with uproarious laughter. Lyle raised his fists in triumph, looking round at them.

Æthelstan raised a hand of his own. 'That's enough fighting for one night, gentlemen. Save it for London.'

Two other Brits had helped John off the table and taken him up to his room.

Things had calmed down after that, and after dinner came brandy and cigars. The smokers were not obliged to go outdoors.

'You're free men. Free to give yourselves lung cancer,

if that's your wish – and all your secondary neighbours, even my dogs!'

Æthelstan lit a fat Romeo Y Julieta Churchill and used it as a prop. He gestured with it, held it to his mouth as he talked, clamped it between the V of his fingers, like the man it was named after, admired the lengthening tip of ash, but Bond noticed that he rarely actually drew on it.

It was growing late, and the guests were starting to drift away to their beds when Æthelstan lead the die-hards out onto a terrace, where gas burners had been lit to keep the guests warm. There were a drinks trolley, tables and chairs, and a few recliners, kitted out with blankets.

The rain had dried up and it was a clear, starlit night, chilled and pleasantly fresh after the raucous, overheated hall. Bond, who had declined a cigar, poured himself a glass of 18-year-old Aberlour from a well-stocked drinks cart. He wasn't too fussy about his whiskies. He enjoyed their variety and abided by the old saying "Any scotch bought with someone else's money is good."

He went to stand by a low wall looking out over the dark countryside, the lights of the scattered houses twinkling as if auditioning for a Disney movie. The terrace had been built on a spur of rock, and, by leaning out a little, Bond was able to get a good view of the lower levels of the castle. There were more windows down there, indicating perhaps another four floors below the one he was on. There was a lot more to the castle than what they'd so far been shown.

'Quite a speech, eh?' Bond was joined by Lord Bonkers,

smoking a comically long cigar. 'The man is certainly an inspiring orator. And not too heavy. Some good laughs. I was thinking about all that footage of Hitler at various rallies and what have you. All very rousing. But he does go on a bit. Often think he could've sugared the pill with a few jokes. Germans famously don't have a sense of humour, you see. Not like the English. A sense of humour is about the most important thing an Englishman can possess. A sense of humour, a sense of decency, a sense of fair play. Freedom and tolerance. It's fashionable to knock the Empire, but we exported all those great qualities in exchange for the imports of goods and services and what have you. People forget that.'

'Yes,' said Bond. 'I suppose they do.'

'Indeed . . . indeed . . .'

Bond let his words hang there. Not saying anything more. Not wanting to give the man any fuel to continue this tedious conversation. He suddenly felt deathly tired. Tired of all this. Angry that he'd had to sit through that damned, boring speech.

The aristocrat shuffled about. Tapped his ash over the wall.

'I'll tell you something,' he said. 'If nothing else, perhaps Æthelstan can bring back good old imperial measurements, eh? Hahaha.'

'Yes,' said Bond wearily. 'It'd be worth it just for that.'

Apart from using miles, Bond had never known imperial measurements. Pounds and ounces, feet and inches, shillings and thruppenny bits and guineas, meant nothing to him. What did he care? The metric system seemed to make a lot more sense. But that wasn't what this twit wanted to hear.

Bond kept silent, waiting for the lord to get bored and move on. He soon did and was replaced by Ragnheiður, who was artfully draped in one of the blankets, as if it was a piece of haute couture.

'So, what did you make of that?' she asked. 'Your first exposure to the King of Wessex.'

'The man is certainly an inspiring orator,' said Bond, keeping a straight face. 'And not too heavy. Some good laughs.'

'You don't believe that, do you?'

'Not a word of it. How about you?'

'I think that the thing he loves most in the world is the sound of his own voice.'

'You must have had to listen to a great many wind-bags over the years,' said Bond. 'From all points of the political compass.'

'I have,' said Ragnheiður. 'And do you know, a boring communist is just as tedious as a boring fascist. Khrushchev's famous "Secret Speech"? Four hours. He could have summed it up in four words – "Stalin was a bastard". Castro? Four hours was nothing to him. Hitler's speech in the Reichstag, 1939 – two and a half hours.'

'And no jokes,' said Bond. Ragnheiður gave him a dark look.

'Boring men love to talk,' she said. 'Most of them prefer words to actions. I can put up with Æthelstan, though, because he's actually planning to do something.'

Bond turned and looked at Ragnheiður's profile. She

was staring out into the dark, seeing something that was invisible to him.

'Ah – there you are.' Æthelstan's rich baritone carried on the still night air. 'Making friends with our little witch, are you? She's a deep one, Sanbourne, let me tell you. You don't want to get tangled up with her.'

He shook Bond's hand. 'I'm glad to finally meet you face to face. First of all, I must thank you for helping Marina out, and then I must thank you for joining our little operation. Getting you and your men on board is the final piece that completes our package. Particularly as an American group I had my sights on pulled out at the last minute.'

'Lucky for me,' said Bond.

'Lucky for you.'

Not luck at all. Some carefully placed misinformation, courtesy of MI6, had scared the Americans off.

Æthelstan nodded to Ragnheiður.

'Shouldn't you be pulling the legs off some spiders?'

Ragnheiður sighed and wandered off towards the drinks trolley.

Æthelstan turned his attention back to Bond.

'Now we're all ship-shape we can set sail, Mister Sanbourne. Operation 848 is all systems go. I'm running this along secret network lines, through discrete cells. None of them briefed on what the other cells are tasked with. So if anything goes wrong for one of them, they can't ruin it for any of the others. That's why I'm keeping you all in ignorance apart from what you need to know to pull off your part of the plan.'

That was smart. Because it meant that none of Æthelstan's mercenaries knew the overall picture. They couldn't judge the wider chances of success. They would trust that the other units would make this thing work.

'Under 848, we have, for instance, Operation Aunty, Operation White Dragon, Operation Long Tom, Operation Slaughterhouse, Operation Æthelflæd, Operation Old Lady . . . Which is where you come in, Sanbourne.'

'Yes. As I understand it, I'll be hitting the City of London.'

'Bank of England. Full and final briefing tomorrow.'

'Can you trust them all?' Bond asked.

'Can I trust you, Mister Sanbourne?'

'As long as you keep paying my bills.'

'Is that all? Do you really care nothing for what our undertaking means?'

'Well . . .' Bond took a step closer to Æthelstan, looking searchingly into his eyes. 'I think it goes beyond England, Æthelstan, which I guess is why so many non-Brits have signed on. The whole system needs shaking up. The world needs a wakeup call. The old ways don't work anymore. The model's broken. As you say, a metropolitan elite has seized power and is trying to impose its twisted, politically correct values on the ordinary people. It's time for something else. It's time for a new way forward.'

Bond stepped back. For a moment he'd almost believed his words. Sometimes an agent went so deep undercover they drowned. They began to believe their cover story and went slowly and quietly insane.

People like Æthelstan had a dangerous talent; they

knew how to harness the power of the disaffected, the disenfranchised.

'Bravo!' Æthelstan was beaming at Bond. 'Well said, that man. I think you've put the argument very well for why so many disparate groups were keen to join in on this. And to answer your question, no, I can't trust them all. Some I could trust to the gates of hell and back, because they know I'm the only man who can make their dreams come true. What a mixed bunch they are, though. Some of them are professionals, like you. Others are hunting dogs. Almost wild. They'll as soon turn on each other as on their prey. Which is why they need a pack leader with a firm whip hand. I'll be glad when Operation 848 is done, and I can let them loose.'

'And what about you, Æthelstan? What if you fail?'

'Did they arrest Trump for the Capitol riots? Is Putin behind bars? Assad? There are enough people out there who want to protect me, Sanbourne. And, whatever happens, it's only a matter of time before I'm accepted, because I speak the truth and I hold the power. People talk of speaking truth to power – I prefer to speak the truth with power.'

Now, lying here in his room in the dark, Bond vividly recalled Æthelstan's face. Beaming with an inner fire. But it wasn't the face of a crazed fanatic, a demagogue foaming at the mouth. He'd just looked smug and supercilious. Like a man who knew something you didn't and was enjoying a joke at your expense.

Bond's thoughts were interrupted by a soft knocking. He wondered if he might have imagined it, or whether it was just the old building creaking, or a branch tapping against a window. And then it came again. There was definitely somebody at his door. He switched on his bedside lamp and checked his watch. It was almost one fifteen. He went cautiously to the door.

'Yes?'

'Are you going to open this door or are you going to keep me standing out here in the cold all night?' A girl's voice. Accented. It could only be Ragnheiður.

'Wait a moment.'

Bond hastily slipped on an old t-shirt and a pair of cotton, drawstring sleep pants.

When he opened the door, Ragnheiður was leaning against the frame with her arms crossed. She was wearing a kimono style dressing gown, apparently naked underneath it, her hair held up by a Japanese kanzashi hair clip decorated with fake flowers.

'I'm not sure it's the done thing for a young girl to go knocking at a strange man's door at this time of the night,' said Bond and she made a face at him.

'No,' she said. 'It's definitely not the done thing.' She pushed the door back and brushed past Bond into the room. Once inside, she closed the door and turned the key in the lock.

Now she took in the room.

'They've put you in one of the good ones,' she said. 'Most of the rooms in this place are rat holes. The castle's falling apart. Æthelstan's good at putting on a front.'

As she spoke, she stalked around the space, picking

up ornaments and looking at the pictures on the walls. Bond stood there patiently, watching her progress.

'What is it you want, exactly?' he asked, keeping the question flat and neutral. Ragnheiður stopped and turned her intense gaze on him. Her eyes flashing. Her ugly beautiful face looking bewitchingly feline.

'What does any girl want in a man's bedroom at night?' she said. 'Don't make me pretend I'm scared of the thunder and want to crawl under the safety of your bedclothes. Because there isn't any storm, I'm not scared of thunder, and I don't need you to protect me.'

'You're a fast worker,' said Bond.

Ragnheiður made a dismissive noise. 'We don't have time to get to know each other,' she said, approaching him and placing a hand on his t-shirt. 'And, in our line of work, weeks of dating and lasting relationships are not really possible, are they? You're a good-looking man, and I'm a good-looking woman. Why wait?'

'What if I were to tell you that I'm in a relationship back in England?'

'Then I would tell you to put it aside and forget about it for one night. You know the saying – "What happens in a remote, crumbling castle in the northern forests of Hungary, stays in a remote, crumbling castle in the northern forests of Hungary."'

'You know, I thought you were perhaps with Canner,' said Bond.

'Why did you think that?'

'Because you seem to hate each other.'

'Ha-ha. We use each other sometimes.'

'And they say romance is dead.'

Ragnheiður leaned in, snaked her arms around Bond's neck and kissed him. He didn't resist, but neither did he give anything back.

'Do you find that difficult?' she said softly. 'To taste another man on my lips? Do you find that *distasteful*?'

'Did you find the taste of another woman on my lips distasteful?'

'I quite like the taste. I'm not particular. If something is beautiful, I want to possess it.'

She tightened her grip on him now and urged him towards the bed. Bond pushed back. She pushed back harder. He pulled her arms from around his neck, twisted her round and pressed one of her wrists into the small of her back.

'Not so fast,' he said into the crook of her shoulder. 'It's late. Whatever it is you want to do, you'll have to . . .' But before he could finish the sentence, Ragnheiður pulled off a perfect self-defence move. In one movement, too fast for Bond to get prepared, she bent at the knees, dropped her shoulder, corkscrewed her arm and twisted her body round so that she was facing him and then powered into his groin, grabbing him round the thighs, and finally, with unexpected strength, she drove upwards, lifting him off the floor and throwing him back onto the bed.

And then she jumped, landing on top of him and straddling his chest with her bare legs. The next moment, she grabbed his hair and pinned his head to the sheets. Her other hand jabbed at his neck, pressing her thumb and first finger into his throat either side of his chin with a strong grip. Then she leant forward and bit one ear, holding it tight between her teeth.

'Just stop,' she hissed. 'Don't be a fool. I'm here to help.'

Bond went limp. All resistance ceased. She let go of his ear and straightened up, looking down at him with a wild look on her face. Panting with the exertion. Her hair dishevelled. Her kimono gaping open.

Then, with another swift, athletic movement, she rolled off him, snatched up the chair from by the desk, and planted it by the door. Once she was satisfied, she stepped back, staring up at a light fitting over the door.

Bond propped himself up on his elbows and watched the show. Wondering where this was going.

'This is not for you, you dirty voyeurs,' she shouted up at the light. 'Go back to watching Pornhub.'

With that, she leaped onto the chair, tore off her kimono and flung it over the light. That must be where the CCTV camera was hidden.

Naked as a nymph in a Victorian painting, Ragnheiður jumped down from the chair, and, laughing, ran back to the bed where she threw herself down next to James and pressed her mouth to his ear. He felt her breath, warm and moist, as she whispered to him.

'Don't get any ideas, handsome. You really think I came here to seduce you? You're so vain. Shh. Don't speak. I just came here to tell you – you and me, we're both the same.'

Bond turned to look at her. Her face so close to his, the eyes shining and wide. He was aware of the length of her body pressed against his. The soft curves of her flesh, buttery in the dim light.

Now she unclipped the kanzashi from her hair and extracted something from it. A small piece of rolled-up paper. She took his hand and pressed the paper into it.

'You read this,' she whispered. 'While I pretend we're behaving like two animals in a wildlife documentary.' She gave him a wide grin, showing her teeth and she kissed him quickly on the lips again.

'Eyes on the paper, handsome.'

He turned over the other way and began unravelling the slip of paper, aware of her getting up behind him. And then he felt the mattress move as she began to jump up and down like a demented teenager at a sleepover who's overdosed on too much blue slushy. Grunting and moaning and shouting out, 'Oh, Peter. Yes, Peter. Peter, you're so good . . .'

Bond tried to ignore her as he read what she'd written.

He gave a long, low whistle.

If he was to believe her, she was playing the same dangerous game as him. Only in her case, it was a long game. His reading of her had been way off. He'd imposed a well-worn story onto her. The story he wanted to believe. In reality, her shift to the right had been a front. A pose. All she'd wanted was to get close to power, to work her way into the dark heart of the far-right organisations that were spreading through Europe like a virus. Æthelstan, as a magnet for these groups, drawing them all into his orbit, was the big prize. He looked round at her. She was kneeling on the bed, now, hugging one of his pillows and smothering it with noisy kisses. She looked at him and winked. He smiled and shook his head.

She was quite a number. So far, she'd managed to keep herself above suspicion, but she wasn't sure how much longer she could last.

Could he trust her, though? Could she be laying an elaborate trap for him? Could this be a set-up? Was Canner testing him? He beckoned her closer with a crooked finger.

'Why have you given me this?' he murmured.

Her expression changed, darkened, and she whispered one word: 'Persimmon'.

Bond swallowed. Persimmon was 009's secret signal. The equivalent of a safe word. All Double O agents had one. Kept it buried deep. You would go to your grave keeping it secret. Die rather than tell it to anyone you didn't absolutely trust. Even if they'd tortured 009 day and night – and judging by the state of his body, they had done – he would never give it up. It was only fellow agents who knew you even had a secret signal. And they had learned each other's. Outside of their tiny circle, the very idea of the signal was totally secret. You would only tell it to someone in a dire emergency.

Ragnheiður was still very close to him.

'Tom told me,' she whispered. A hint of sadness in her voice. Tom Ferguson had been 009's alias for the mission. 'And he told me that others would come. He described them all so that I would recognise you. I know who you are. You're James Bond.'

Bond realised that Ragnheiður had put the pillow down and he hadn't been the slightest bit aware of her nakedness. His head was in a different place. And she, for her part, was totally unselfconscious. Nevertheless, he pulled his t-shirt off over his head and handed it to her. He looked away to give her some privacy as she put it on.

'Tell me,' he said, as quietly as he could. 'Does D37 mean anything to you?'

She nodded.

It's her, he thought. 009 had given the information to her.

Bond's mind was racing. Just where the hell did he go from here?

April 12th – 24 days
until the Coronation

Bond nodded to the man who was waiting for him at the entrance to the compound where Æthelstan's PMC grunts were assembled. The two of them had been through a lot together over the years and Bond was always reassured to see him. There's a special trust that forms between two people who have faced death together. This was perhaps going to be their most dangerous undertaking yet. Shutting down Æthelstan's operation was not going to be easy. If anyone could do it, Captain Nick Cornwell and his squad were the best men for the job.

Like many officers, particularly in the elite units, Captain Cornwell was slightly built and anonymous looking. Very different to the image of a hulking, meat-head berserker that many people pictured when they heard the phrase 'special forces'. But Bond knew all too well what lay beneath Cornwell's mild, trim exterior. The man was tougher than a tungsten hammer. He stood there patiently on the other side of the security barrier. Arms folded. Expression neutral. Cornwell was an ex-marine. And soldiers were used to waiting.

Bond had shown his ID card and accreditation to the guards at the gate, and one of them was in the security hut telephoning up to the castle. The compound was surrounded by three parallel rows of razor wire fences. Whether this was to keep the men in, or to keep outsiders out wasn't clear. But Æthelstan clearly wasn't taking any chances.

Presently the guard came out of his hut, gave Bond his documents and waved him through as the barrier tilted up.

'Morning, sir,' said Cornwell politely.

'Morning, captain,' said Bond and they set off, side by side, through the camp. 'All well?'

'All well, sir. The last of the lads finally arrived this morning. Most of them are on the firing range. We can talk there. Zero chance of being overheard.'

'Very good.'

After clearing in the night, and a brief, glorious burst of sun first thing, the bad weather had returned, a gunmetal grey sky overhung the castle, and the day was cold and wet. The ground, churned up by vehicles and heavy boots, was slushy and pitted with muddy puddles.

The camp was busy with Æthelstan's men moving in and out of the bunk buildings. More men were sitting under makeshift shelters on crates, drinking cups of tea or coffee. Chatting in the desultory manner of people on downtime. There was an edge to the lassitude, though, an air of tension. All these men, from seasoned mercenaries to fanatics drunk on a warped idealism, were cooped up here together getting ready for a mission, the outcome of which was far from certain.

And Cornwell's men had a secret mission of their own. To turn this whole thing on its head. Bond could feel his stomach tightening already, his skin crawling. It was going to be one hell of a brawl. He and Cornwell passed a large tent with open sides, where a group of men were being briefed. Bond recognised a couple of the men doing the talking. Like himself, they'd been at the dinner last night.

As they came to the substation, Bond glanced over. Assessing it quickly and expertly. It was the prime target of their mission. Harry 'H' Lascelles was the explosives expert in Cornwell's group. He'd know exactly where to put the charges to cause maximum damage. Bond hoped they had access to all the ordinance they needed here in the camp.

Cornwell was aware of Bond's attention and knew what he was thinking.

'We've found access to the explosives. H's unit are briefed. They'll break into the depot as soon as everything kicks off. They know exactly which bits of equipment to target.'

'Good.'

A Polaris 4x4 LMV with three uniformed men on board rocked past, bouncing on the uneven ground. With its open sides and skeletal build, it looked like a militarised golf buggy. The Polaris was followed by a dirty truck that deliberately swerved to drive through a deep puddle in an attempt to splash Bond and Cornwell.

The two men jumped back in unison and avoided the worst of the spray.

Someone laughed. Someone else made a raucous comment. Bond offered a rueful smile and pressed on.

He glanced down at his overcoat, which was now spotted with muddy water. He was wearing it for the first time since playing cat and mouse with Ragnheiður in Budapest. As he thrust his hands into his pockets, he felt something unfamiliar, and it took him a moment to realise it was the little parcel of smoked paprika he'd bought for Yasmin. As he ran his fingers over the smoothness of the paper packaging, he thought how pathetic it seemed and felt a hollow pang of loneliness. This sad, little item was a reminder of a distant, bland domesticity. It was an unwelcome intrusion from another world.

Bond became aware of the sound of muffled gunfire and Cornwell explained that the shooting range had been built inside the hill, in a bunker at the end of an old tunnel that had been dug and fitted out in the war. There were two more guards stationed at the entrance to the tunnel. Bond had to once again show his ID. Cornwell, too.

The guards let them through, their petty moment of power momentarily lifting the boredom of their day. Bond and Cornwell entered the tunnel and walked over to where a box of ear defenders sat on a trestle table. The noise of gunfire was considerably louder than it had been outside, slamming and rattling off the walls, and as they walked deeper into the hillside, Bond and Cornwell slipped the ear mufflers on.

The walls were lined with concrete and cheap stone, stained with damp and mould and streaked with rust.

After about 100 metres the tunnel opened out into a wider space off which five smaller tunnels radiated, and it was in these that the targets had been set up for practise. Under the watchful eye of Æthelstan's ever-present security, Cornwell's men were taking their turn on the range. Firing Glock side arms, various sub-machine guns, and heavier SA80s at the targets.

Cornwell eased his defender off one ear and Bond did likewise.

'They're trying out auto sears on the Glocks,' Cornwell shouted over the noise.

'And?' Bond had heard about auto sears. Cheap plastic devices, that, when fitted into the back of the pistols turned them into machine guns.

'Maximum impact, minimum accuracy. They're insane.'

Bond looked over at a group of Cornwell's men, who were evidently fascinated by the impact an auto sear made. He'd described the unit he was supplying to Canner Lyle as disgruntled ex-military, and so they were. Mostly SAS, SBS, and Royal Marines. The closest to the truth that you can make a cover story, the better. But it was MI6 who had scooped them up and given them a fresh purpose in life, before they were tempted to join any more renegade outfits. Some of them had been in the SRR before being taken under M's wing.

Bond stood back with Cornwell, as if the two of them were discussing training.

'So, how is it all going down here in camp?' he asked.

'To be honest, sir, it's a shitshow. It's getting pretty toxic. Worse every day. A lot of the guys Æthelstan's pulled together aren't properly trained. They're street thugs. It causes a lot of friction with the military. And the biggest problem is the other Brits. They're displaying all the prejudices of a certain type of British nugget. Can't stand the foreign PMCs. There was a fight last night between some of the French and John Tyler's mob. And the South Africans aren't helping. Strutting about trying to lord it up over everyone else. They reckon they're the only professionals here. They're professionals, all right, but they're also nutters, a right bunch of tough bastards.'

'Do you reckon you can push things over the edge?' Bond had to raise his voice but was confident that nobody standing more than a metre away would be able to hear a word.

'Shouldn't be too difficult. There's not to supposed to be any booze in camp, but somehow the Brits have got hold of some and have set up a black-market, flogging the stuff to the other guys at vastly inflated rates. There's also a flourishing trade in puff and powder. All ingredients for a wild party. We've identified the chief troublemakers, the guys most likely to kick off, and set up a whispering campaign. It's not gonna take much to light the spark and then this place is gonna go up like a box of fireworks.'

'Looks like we're both as ready as we'll ever be.'

'Do you have all the intel you need, sir?'

'As a matter of fact, I have. A little bird told me.'

Cornwell smiled. 'I won't ask.'

'The reason Æthelstan needs all that extra power is

109

because, not only has he got a major broadcasting centre set up in the castle, but he's also running some heavy-duty computing with seriously chunky mainframes.'

'But what's it all for?'

'*Everything's* digital these days, Nick. Especially warfare. He's going to be waging a digital war as well as a physical one. The man started his professional life as a trader in the City. That's still where the bulk of his wealth is coming from. He's built himself a mini-trading centre up there, apparently. We've got to get in there and shut it down, pronto.'

'How pronto?'

'I'd love to say we have all the time in the world, but I'd be lying. They don't trust me up there, and with things the way they are down here, I want to get this thing over with on my terms. We make our move tomorrow.'

Cornwell's mouth made the shape of a long whistle, but Bond could near nothing over the din from the range.

'We'll have to synchronise so that you hit the substation at the same time as I hit Æthelstan,' he went on. 'He'll have backup generators, but there's going to have to be a switch over. A slight delay between the main power supply being cut and the secondary backup supply coming onstream. It'll be a small window but it's all I'll have. I'm counting on you, Nick.'

'For King and Country, sir,' said Cornwell with irony. 'I'm here to serve. What are the protocols? Maximum force?'

Cornwell was a soldier. He understood about service. As did Bond. They'd both been in service all their working lives. First under Her Majesty Queen Elizabeth II, and now under King Charles III.

A soldier was not like other men. A soldier agreed to a special contract.

Most people misunderstood the terms. The contract a soldier made was not that he was prepared to *die* for his country – although that must always be a possibility – it was that he was prepared to *kill* for his country.

'Deadly force,' said Bond. 'You do what you have to do, and I'll do what *I* have to do. But once you've switched on the Christmas lights down here, you have to get up top. I'll need you to help me shut down his operation.'

'Not going to be easy.'

'Tell me something I don't know, Nick.'

'Dolly Parton's real name is Dolly.'

'Never knew that. Always thought it was a nickname.'

Two of Æthelstan's security came over. Bond and Cornwell nodded to them as they were given an appraising look.

'Well, Captain Cornwell,' said Bond. 'This all looks in order. Keep on carrying on.'

'Yes, sir.'

As they walked down the tunnel and back through the camp to the gates, Bond had just enough time to fill Cornwell in on the fine detail and the timings. Even as he said it, spelling it out in stark black and white, it sounded desperately thin and forlorn. Just as Æthelstan's attack on London was doomed to failure, Bond's attack on Æthelstan sounded equally, recklessly foolhardy.

It was going to be hairy, and Bond had had so many

111

close shaves, he wasn't sure he had any skin left on his teeth.

Outside, the sky was black and starless. The flicker of lightning over the distant mountains was like a migraine coming on. Bond turned away from his bedroom window and went back to pacing the room. He was still fully clothed. Sleep was an impossibility. His mind was turning too fast. He'd been trying to ignore the three decanters sitting, beguilingly, on a side table – whisky, gin and brandy.

He checked his watch. It was nearly 3:30 a.m. It was going to be a long night.

He swore, and walked quickly over to the table. Half-filled a crystal glass with whisky and downed a hefty slug. Anything to slow his brain and still the shivers in his gut.

He kept coming back to the feeling that his plan was as insane as Æthelstan's and wishing for the thousandth time that he had a proper weapon. He toyed with the idea of sneaking down to the entrance hall and trying to retrieve his Glock from the plastic box in its cubby hole, but there were too many risks involved. Too many cameras. As far as he could tell, the entrance hall was guarded day and night. Ragnheiður had filled him in on as much information as she could, including what 009 had been able to learn before they killed him. It still wasn't enough, though. There were too many gaps in his knowledge. People had laughed at Donald Rumsfeld for his 'known unknowns' and 'unknown unknowns', but Bond knew exactly what he'd been talking about.

His head was filled with unknown unknowns.

Still, he might not have his Glock, but he had something.

He retrieved his suitcase from the cradle where the servants had left it and wheeled it over to the wardrobe as if he was putting it away out of sight. He opened the wardrobe door and angled it so that the camera hidden in the light fitting wouldn't be able to see what he was doing and quickly extended the telescopic handle to its full length. He then opened the case and felt for the hidden button that released the handle from the body of the suitcase. In one quick, practised move, he pulled the handle free, detached one of the poles and slipped it out of its sheath. It ended in a vicious point. It was crude and limited, but it was pretty much all he had. He slid it up his sleeve and secured the point behind his watch strap. Now he was as prepared as he could be for whatever might happen.

He went back to his pacing. Waiting for the minutes to tick away.

After visiting Cornwell at the camp, he'd had a briefing in a small meeting room with Æthelstan and Canner Lyle. It had been like any dull, business conference. They might have been planning a takeover bid for a rival accountancy firm. With the help of diagrams, spreadsheets, maps, and Google Street View, Æthelstan had painstakingly walked Bond through his small part of Operation 848 – 'Operation Old Lady'.

'The Old Lady of Threadneedle Street – the Bank of England. You've been given the cherry, Sanbourne.'

'A juicy target, admittedly,' said Bond. 'But built to withstand a lot more than we can throw at it.'

'I'm not expecting your squad to actually get inside, Sanbourne. You'd need a tank to do that. I just need you to disrupt things, to create a panic, to shut the city down. At the same time that you hit the Old Lady, other cells will be hitting Lloyds, the Stock Exchange and St Paul's.'

'So, let me get this straight, you're not actually expecting any of your units to succeed in getting inside anywhere?'

'Getting in is irrelevant. Did you see the footage of the Capitol riots? All those good old boys storming in with their beer bellies sagging over their belts? When they got inside, it was perfectly comical! They hadn't a clue what to do. They'd got in – now what? They wiped their fat white arses on some documents, put their feet up on the speaker's desk. They hadn't expected to ever get in, and, when they did – *now what*? The enormity of the situation pole-axed them. There's a great deal more to bringing down a government than breaking into a building. They were like bunch of baboons who'd escaped from their cage in a zoo and got into the zookeepers' offices. Throwing their shit about. Making lots of noise . . . but there was no way they were ever going to wind up running the zoo.

'But I am not a baboon. I am prepared and organised and well-funded. We already have people on the inside, Sanbourne. Everywhere! Waiting for the flag to go up. Even at the palace. And we have a back-up plan. You must always have a back-up plan. If things are looking grim, then Operation Æthelflæd will be put into effect. They chopped Charles's ancestor's head off. The *first*

King Charles. It was controversial, yes, but hugely popular at the time.'

Æthelstan laughed uproariously, and Canner joined in. 'So, you leave that side of things to me. You don't have to worry your pretty little head about it. You are boots on the ground, Sanbourne. You will not need to put them up on anybody's desk. And you don't need to know what wider plans are being hatched at HQ.'

'I just hope my men and I aren't going to end up as cannon fodder,' said Bond.

'You're all grown-ups. You can look after yourselves. But I have an exit plan for you. An escape route. For all of you . . .'

The escape route was plausible enough but relied on too many things going exactly to plan. Bond knew from bitter experience that any military plan started to go wrong as soon as it was put into effect.

Luckily, he didn't have to worry about any of that, though. His action was all going to take place here in the castle.

He stopped pacing. There had been a knock on the door. He took a deep breath and strode over.

'What is it? It's late.'

'Not too late for me, surely.' Ragnheiður's voice was husky and seductive. Bond felt a cold flush of apprehension through his body. He opened the door. There she stood, fully clothed this time and with a slightly furtive, nervous look about her. In a moment it was clear why. From either side of the door, four men appeared.

Æthelstan and Canner Lyle from one side. Kenny

Charlton and an armed guard from the other. Both brandishing short-barrelled G36s with the buttstocks folded.

Bond caught Ragnheiður's eye. She looked away.

Lyle came forward, forcing Bond back into the room. The others followed, Ragnheiður bringing up the rear. Lyle backed Bond up to one of the bedposts. Bond stood there, holding Lyle's hot stare. They were intimately close. Bond saw that Canner was wearing his ubiquitous, oversized ear buds, and he could just hear a faint, tinny buzz and beat.

Lyle smiled, and reached down to cup Bond's testicles in his right hand. Gently at first. Almost a caress.

Bond broke away from the staring contest and looked over at the others. Kenny and the guard had their weapons aimed steadily at him, the muzzles like two black eyes. Ragnheiður looked flushed, excited. Æthelstan, grim-faced, accusing.

Lyle put his mouth close to Bond's ear.

'You think you've got bigger balls than me, Bond?' There it was. He'd used his real name. Ragnheiður had told him. 'Nobody has bigger balls then me.'

'I find that hard to believe,' said Bond. 'Everybody knows that anabolic steroid abuse shrinks your testes.'

'Funny man, huh?' Canner started to tighten his grip, sending a numbing pain up through Bond's body. 'By the time I've finished with you, you won't have any balls, buddy.'

There was a sick feeling in Bond's stomach. His head felt like it was going to explode.

'Save it,' said Æthelstan. 'You can have your fun with

116

him later. Let's get him out of here and into somewhere more secure.'

Canner grabbed Bond by his jacket, pulled him across the room and shoved him roughly out of the door. Ragnheiður came out and gave Bond a long, cold look. Canner kissed her fiercely.

'You did well, baby.' Turning to Bond. 'And you failed, buddy.'

They marched Bond down the corridor, through a door that led into a staff access corridor, then along to a service lift. Canner lifted his lanyard and pressed his plastic ID card to the reader.

The lift was steel-walled and functional. Brightly lit by fluorescents in the ceiling. Canner used his ID card again and pressed the lowest button on the floor selector panel. The lift sank into the bowels of the castle – one floor, two floors, three floors, four floors.

Bond could see himself reflected in the warped steel of the lift. A distorted, ugly shape. The skin sallow under the harsh lighting. Like something out of a Francis Bacon painting. When the lift came to a halt, the doors slid open and the guard manhandled Bond out. There was a network of old tunnels down here. Perhaps they once connected dungeons or storage cellars, or they might be more recent additions, like the tunnels at the foot of the hill, built during the war.

They had to pass through another security door and Canner impatiently went through the ritual with his ID card. Then they were passing along a high, enclosed walkway, a sort of bridge, with reinforced glass walls.

It crossed over the top of what looked like a city trading floor. Busy even at this time of night. It no doubt ran around the clock, accessing every market and stock exchange in the world. Ragnheiður had been telling the truth when she'd described this part of the castle. There must have been 20 or 30 people down there, excitedly studying monitors, or looking up at the trading display that covered an entire wall. It was like a casino in Vegas. No windows or natural light to give any indication of whether it was day or night. A casino owner had once told him that "Money exists outside time."

Bond looked at the list of data on the big screen. The workings of the market were all a mystery to him.

No one bothered to glance up as the little group made its way over their heads and through another security door. They were now back in the old part of the castle, in a tunnel carved out of the solid rock. They turned a corner, opened another door and then Bond found himself unexpectedly being shoved into a brightly lit TV studio.

Three pedestal-mounted robot cameras turned to watch him come in, like curious, one-eyed creatures. Bond had been in a couple of automated studios before, where everything was remotely controlled. No need for cameramen. There was a presenting area, a seating area with brightly coloured sofas and a low table, and a bigger, circular table with chairs around it in a third area.

The wall was a wide, curved semi-circle with a grid pattern on it. In a virtual studio like this, computers would fill in any background you wanted.

Lyle frogmarched Bond to a black office chair

standing in the centre of the presenting area and sat him down.

'So, did you enjoy having my sweet Ragnheiður in your room, Bond? Stealing all your secrets?'

'I don't know what the silly, scheming little bitch has been telling you, Canner. But aren't you going to let me have my say?'

'No, I'm not. Did you really think she really wanted to rut with you? She's *my* bitch, Bond.'

Canner nodded to Ragnheiður and tossed her a bundle of cable ties. She came round behind Bond, roughly jerked his hands behind his back and secured his wrists to the chrome back support with a single tie. Canner was circling him, watching Ragnheiður work, enjoying it. When she was done, he put his thick, meaty arm round Bond's neck and squeezed, cutting off the blood flow to his head and the air flow to his lungs. Bond's face felt hot and tight with trapped blood. His brain fizzed and his vision was clouded with bright dots.

'I could break your neck and pull your head off if I wanted,' said Canner. Bond could smell the man's body. A musky stink of dried sweat and glandular secretions. He passed out, the blackness of oblivion hitting him like a hammer blow.

He had no idea how long he was out for, but his head jerked him awake as it straightened up. The torn muscles hurt like hell. He looked around the studio, waiting for his vision to clear. He felt sick as a cat but wasn't going to give Canner the satisfaction of seeing him puke.

119

And now the big South African took out a folding knife and opened its wide, curved blade.

'So, where shall we start?' he said.

'What is it you want from me?' said Bond.

'You're going to star in our very first broadcast, Mister Bond,' said Æthelstan. 'We can learn a lot from the likes of Isis. Like the value of a good propaganda video. Shared and shared and shared again all around the world.

'This little film will let your masters know just how badly you failed. How badly *they* failed. How puny they will look on the world stage. We've prepared a little confession for you to make.' As he spoke, Kenny led over a camera with an autocue attachment on the front. Bond ran his eyes over the first few lines.

My name is James Bond. I am an agent of the deep state. Of the one world government. I am a hired killer. I was sent to illegally murder an innocent civilian . . .

'You expect me to read this?' he said dismissively.

'Yes. Once we've softened you up.'

'What are you going to do, play one of your tedious speeches on a loop until I crack?'

'Oh, you're so amusing, Mister Bond. But I can assure you, Canner can be very persuasive. His reputation precedes him.'

With that, Canner lashed out with a foot, kicking Bond in the chest, and sending him rolling away across the studio floor, still attached to the chair. The cameras following his progress. Kenny yelped with laughter.

'Good shot, boss,' he said.

Bond took a deep breath in and let it out slowly,

assessing the damage. Nothing serious had been done to his chest. The chair flying back had taken the force out of the kick.

Canner nodded to Ragnheiður and she wheeled Bond back onto his mark.

'Hold him still this time.'

'What are you going to—'

Bond's words were brutally cut off as Canner delivered a whip-fast kick to his left knee. Pain shot up and down his leg and he clenched his teeth waiting for it to pass. He remembered seeing the sickening photographs of 009's body. How it had been covered in bruises. Canner must have beaten him all over, using fists and feet and elbows. Starting by bruising the flesh and moving on to breaking the bones. One by one. But always careful to leave his victim alive. It wasn't subtle or clever. It was an act of blunt savagery. 009 had been preternaturally brave. He hadn't broken. Hadn't told Æthelstan anything. Bond wondered just how brave *he* was. How long he could hold out before he agreed to read the words on the autocue. He had to play for time. Try to keep Æthelstan talking.

'You can have me beaten to a pulp, Æthelstan,' he said. 'You can force me to read that damned message. But it won't make your crazy plan any more likely to succeed.'

'Oh, really? What makes you think that? Have you written me off as just another mad fanatic?'

'I don't think you're insane, Æthelstan. Far from it. It would be easier to accept you if you were. I think you're a cold, scheming bastard. Which is why I have

121

to ask you – do you *seriously* believe you can sit on the throne of England?'

Æthelstan laughed. 'Do I seriously believe I can sit on the throne of England? No. Of course not. What a ridiculous idea. *I* don't believe it. *You* don't believe it. The only important thing is that *they* believe it. My stout-hearted men of war at the bottom of the hill.'

'So, what's the bloody point of it all?'

'Oh, come along. You don't have to sit on the throne to be in charge, Bond. After all, Charlie-boy doesn't hold any real power. He's a figurehead, a sock puppet, a marketing mascot for the UK. Hell, the British monarchy started to give it all away when King John signed the Magna Carta in 1215.

'Truth is, the government doesn't hold any real power, either. They're at the whim of global forces way beyond their control. So, they tinker with the few things they *can* have an effect on – transport, education, arts funding.

'It's very simple. There's one great power in the world. Money. You know the old saying "Remember the golden rule – he who has the gold makes the rules". Hahahaha!'

Kenny joined in the laughter. 'I've not heard that one before, boss.'

'That's because you're a moron,' said Canner.

'That I am,' said Kenny. 'A happy moron.'

'How I love morons,' said Æthelstan. 'I already have a small army of morons in England. Fanatics, waiting to be activated. The followers of my followers, the likes of John Tyler and Anthony Birkett, the muppets who hang on my every word. And down in my compound, as you well know, I have properly trained, elite troops at my command.'

'You won't even get your men into the country.'

'Do you think a government that can't even stop overloaded rubber dinghies full of illegal immigrants crossing the channel, can stop my boys? Forget the Capitol riots, the disruption is going to be unprecedented! And if anything happens to me, if my grand plan is thwarted, I told you, Mister Bond, I have a backup plan. I'm going to celebrate my birthday whatever happens.'

'I can't wait to see you on the stamps,' said Bond.

'Ha-ha. Yes. Of course, I can't actually, physically, depose Charles . . . *yet*. But I can put the wheels in motion because I have the money. Sooner or later he'll be out on his ear. It may take a year, five years . . . ten. But eventually, I *will be* running the country.'

'Yes, and I'll score the winning goal for England in the next World Cup,' said Bond. 'You'll never convince me that any of this is going to work.'

'You saw my centre of operations when we came here,' said Æthelstan, and Bond could see Canner shifting his weight from one foot to the other, bored, wanting to get on with it. Kenny and the guard had relaxed, their gun barrels drooping. They'd obviously heard one too many of Æthelstan's rants and knew they were in for the long haul.

'You probably surmised that it's a trading floor. A marketplace. Connected to the world. Do you know, I'm one of the few people that didn't take a massive hit when the western economy collapsed in 2008.'

'I'm so happy for you.'

'Please, Bond. Enough with the childish quips. Do you want to know how I made a profit out of others' loss? Because I'm smart. I'm smarter than everyone else. Why, just recently I've made several million out of the collapse of Credit Suisse. A Swiss bank, Bond! Imagine that! A Swiss bank failing. Nobody expected that – except me!

'Most people are still mystified by the crash of 2008. Which means they won't learn from their mistakes. The average man on the street will never understand what happened, or how, or why. And that general ignorance can be exploited. It's easy to lay the blame at the feet of your chosen target – poor people, foreigners, immigrants, liberals, the intelligentsia, Jews . . . And the one big thing that most people don't know is where all the money went. What happened to the billions upon billions of dollars lost by individuals, organisations, cities, countries . . . It didn't all just disappear. It wasn't tossed into a fiery pit and incinerated. Money flows. It circulates like blood. Oh, people think that maybe it went to some other countries? Or maybe a secretive, one world, Global, Jewish, Freemason, Knights Templar, Illuminati organisation stole it all? No, Mister Bond. It all ended up in the hands of individuals. Clever men, who *bet* against the banks. Who bet against countries. *They* personally got hold of all that money. And they're now, if they so desire, in a position to control things.

'As I say, it's quite simple, Mister Bond. You've probably even worked it out for yourself in that unimaginative, little civil service brain of yours.'

'You're betting against the UK.'

'Ta-daa! The penny drops – as does the value of the pound! Yes, I'm shorting the British economy. Everyone is banking on the coronation being a boost for the economy, a chance for the UK to step up in the world. But what if the UK is shown to be a chaotic, badly defended, dangerous, rickety little banana republic? At the mercy of internal forces that want to tear it apart? Well then, the markets crash, the money flows. It will flow into my pockets.'

'You don't care a damn about England.'

'Oh, you're so bloody right. I long ago stopped caring. It's not a country worth caring for anymore. Because it's not a country that cares about itself. About what it once was. It's not a United Kingdom, it's a disunited kingdom. There will be chaos in the markets and when there's chaos there's always a great deal of money to be made. In this case – by me. I have some useful idiots who will run around making a lot of noise and breaking things. And I have some clever men, who have the wherewithal to damage infrastructure and make the country seize up. Grind to a halt. And me? I'll be here. Inviolate. Untouchable. Even if you *had* managed to get a message out, to send for the cavalry, I'm in bed with the Hungarians. It's in Orban's interests to keep me safe.'

'You're war-mongering scum, Æthelstan.'

'You say that as if war's a bad thing.'

Kenny laughed and Æthelstan grinned. Enjoying playing to the crowd.

'I suppose to most people it *is*. They only see war as a bringer of death and destruction and misery, but if you're an arms manufacturer at the start of the First World War, you'll be rubbing your hands together with glee. If you make tanks, 1939 is going to be a bumper year for you. Every time a drone is shot down in the Ukraine, a drone manufacturer pops another bottle of champagne. And covid. My word there was a lot of money to be made from covid. It wouldn't surprise me if some clever man had created that virus and spread it around the world as a way of making a fortune. If I'd had the knowhow, I'd have done it myself. But manipulating the markets is my thing. In times of stability, the markets are stable, so there aren't massive, instant gains to be made. You can only take a long-term view, slow and strong and steady. When the markets are volatile, however, there are huge losses, but those losses are somebody else's gains.'

'All of this just to line your pockets.'

'No, no, no. Far from it. Once Britain is on its knees, it'll need a saviour. A strong man with a vision. As I say, it may take a while, but I will be invited to take charge, eventually. Because I will be the banker in this little game. And the banker always wins. So, now then, why don't you just read your little message and I might find a way to be kind to you.'

'You know I'll never read that garbage.'

'In that case I will have to let Canner continue. Where do you want to start, Mister Lyle? A finger? A kneecap? Or somewhere more personal? Just leave the face untouched.'

'We don't want to spoil the handsome boy,' said Ragnheiður, and she giggled.

Canner advanced on Bond with his knife.

'Please,' said Ragnheiður. 'Let me start?'

Canner grinned and handed her the knife.

'You're a bad girl,' he said.

'That's why you love me.'

Bond spat onto the floor.

'You're just a sad nihilist, Ragnheiður, addicted to seeing things fall.'

'Party on,' said Ragnheiður, and she came round behind Bond, leant over and bit his ear. Hard. Bond winced. Thought she might bite it off this time.

'Stop it. That'll show!' Æthelstan snapped.

'All right. How about I unzip you at the back, Handsome?'

Bond felt the tip of the blade being pushed into the skin at the nape of his neck. It stung and he felt a trickle of blood creep down his back. Ragnheiður started to drag the blade up into his hairline.

'Once he's done his star turn, we should deglove him like we did to that girl in Mogadishu,' said Kenny. 'Peel his face off from the back.'

'You could wear it as a mask, Kenny,' said Ragnheiður. 'Hide that ugly mug of yours.'

Kenny laughed. 'I've a face only a mother could love,' he agreed. 'It's been my fortune. It helps being a right ugly bugger when you want to scare people.' He hung his G36 from its strap over his shoulder and framed his cheeks in his hands, pouting like a starlet posing for a shot.

'Let's get on with this,' said Æthelstan. 'It's nearly

127

four and I want to be back in my bed. Bond? The choice is yours: read the message and sleep. Or resist and enter a whole world of pain.'

'All right. Let's get it over with,' said Bond sourly. 'I'll read your bloody message, Æthelstan. For all the good it'll do you.'

'That's better. Lights, camera, action!'

The cameras swivelled and focused. Bond stared straight down the barrel of the one with the autocue on it.

'Very good,' said Æthelstan. 'For the record, it is 4a.m on the morning of the 13th of April 2023. Over to you, sir.'

Bond filled his lungs, let his breath out slowly, allowing his pounding heart to settle down. Wanting his voice to be strong and clear.

'The name's Bond,' he said. 'James Bond.' The next moment there was an earth-shaking tremor, an almighty thump, and it all went dark.

Things happened quickly after that. Bond felt Ragnheiður slice through the cable tie with the knife. He'd already jiggled the spike hidden up his sleeve loose from his watch strap and he let it slip down into his hand. He'd marked exactly where the guard was standing, calculated the distance, and run through the strike in his mind, like a golfer preparing to drive a ball. As soon as the tie was cut, he was up and out of his chair, gripping the spike in both hands, and lunging at where he knew the guard's chest would be, driving through, aiming for a spot on the other side of the body. There was a dull thud as he hit the man just to the right of his sternum. The man belched obscenely and fell away from him. When the emergency lighting came on a moment later, he was lying dead on the floor, bathed in an infernal red glow.

Bond was still moving. Spinning round. This time his lethal spike was homing in on Kenny, who was fumbling with the gun that was still hanging from its shoulder strap, not yet comprehending what was happening. By the time he realised, it was too late. Once again, the cold, merciless spike struck home. Kenny's harsh bark was the last obscenity to ever come out of his mouth. The spike was jammed between his ribs and he twisted as he fell. It was too slick with blood for Bond to keep a grip on it. He was weapon-less.

Ragnheiður, meanwhile, had moved on Canner. The knife ready to slash at him.

'I'm nobody's bitch,' she snarled.

But Lyle, whose reactions were faster than Kenny's, was ready for her. He slammed the palm of his open right hand into the point of her jaw, causing a shockwave to pass through her head and into her brain, bringing on instant unconsciousness. She fell back heavily and hit the shiny concrete floor with a nasty smack.

Bond quickly assessed the situation. More lights were flickering back on. The backup generators must have come to life and the red light was replaced by a dazzling blaze of white.

Ragnheiður, Kenny and the guard were out of it. Lyle was advancing towards Bond, unarmed. Æthelstan was frozen in shock. Bond was between him and the dead guard. Kenny had fallen closer to him, but he was lying on his G36, and it was tangled in the strap.

Bond had to try to get to the guard's gun. It wasn't going to be easy. Lyle was squaring up to him, bouncing on the balls of his feet, rotating his head on his neck, rolling his shoulders, clenching and unclenching his fists.

He was still wearing his earbuds. Soundtracking the scene like a movie.

Bond had studied videos of the man on YouTube in his cage-fighting days after he left the South African army, trying to spot any weaknesses. He'd come to the conclusion that there weren't any. Canner was very good. He'd proved it last night when he'd taken out John Tyler. He was fast and powerful and ruthless. Deadly with his hands and his feet. You could see that when he went into a fight he had the utter conviction that he was going to win.

And he'd never lost a fight.

Was that, perhaps, a weakness? Overconfidence?

Bond wasn't sure. He knew one thing, however. In a fair fight, Lyle would kill him. Bond didn't intend to fight fair, though. It had to be vicious and underhand if he was to stand a chance. Even in cage fighting there were rules. Did Canner expect Bond to demonstrate the stereotypical Englishman's sense of fair play?

"It's just not cricket, to cheat, old sport."

Bond hated fighting. If a fight started it meant that all else had failed. It was a last resort. Fighting was painful and things got broken. If you did get into a fight, then you had to shut it down as fast as was humanly possible.

Three words came unwanted into his mind.

Headphone. Testosterone. Toblerone.

He pushed them aside. *Concentrate, man.*

Would he have time to get over to the guard, grab his gun, ready it for firing and shoot Lyle before Lyle got to him?

Lyle answered that question for him. He leapt forward, fast as a striking snake, pivoted on his left leg, leaned his upper body over and raised his right leg, making a perfect, flattened Y-shape. Going with the momentum, he wheeled his raised leg round, aiming to smash his foot into Bond's jaw.

It was all Bond could do to jump back and sideways, and he still had to jerk his head back so fiercely that he felt something rip in his neck. If he hadn't got out of the way, though, he'd be as unconscious as Ragnheiður right now. It had been an ugly and clumsy defensive move that wouldn't win you any points in a display match. But he was still standing.

And Lyle was still moving. He cartwheeled his upper leg down and pivoted on it, spinning as he lifted his left leg, and kicked Bond square in the chest.

It was like being hit by a truck. Bond gave a great 'oof!' as the air was driven out of his lungs and he was shunted backwards. He just had the wherewithal to make a safe landing and roll clear of any follow up from Canner.

Æthelstan was fumbling with Kenny, trying to flip him over and untangle the gun.

Bond didn't have long.

He was down. His best hope was to use his position to launch an attack. Remembering how Ragnheiður had made a fool of him in his bedroom, he tipped forward into a squat, planted his feet firmly on the floor and immediately straightened both legs, coming up like a piston and powering his shoulder into Canner's side, just beneath his armpit, as he readied himself for his next fancy move. Canner grunted and staggered back as Bond carried on with his movement, pushing past his opponent and getting clear.

Canner was angry now. He came for Bond in a flurry of punches and kicks. Bond moved in close, getting inside the South African's reach so he couldn't put any energy into his attacks. Bond held up to the pummelling, ignoring it as he dug his right hand into his pocket where his fingers quickly found what they were looking for. He clamped his eyes and mouth shut, held his breath, brought his hand out and slammed it into Canner's face, opening it at the last moment, so that the flimsy, paper package it was holding easily burst.

With his eyes shut, he smelled, rather than saw, the stinging red cloud that erupted around Canner's head. It was a pungent, smoky, fiery smell, and it filled the studio. He moved far enough away from Canner to risk opening his eyes and saw a haze of red powder hanging in the air. Canner, his whole face covered in the stuff, was cursing Bond with the foulest language he could dredge up. He was blinded, gasping, choking, tears streaming down his face and streaking the cloying powder that painted his cheeks. He wiped the back of his hand across his eyes. Which only made it worse. He swore again.

Bond was impressed. He'd never considered using paprika as a weapon before and was amazed at how effective it was.

Canner was blinking, gasping, pushing out his hands in defensive moves and turning on the spot in case Bond came at him.

And Bond did come at him. He backhanded the hard edge of his fist into one of Canner's outsized earbuds. The South African shrieked and clutched the side of his head.

The red dust still hung in the air and a cough alerted Bond to Æthelstan. Damn. He'd forgotten about the man. He had Kenny's gun and was bringing it round on Bond. Bond's gut sense kicked in and he launched himself across the studio a split second before Æthelstan opened fire.

Untrained and acting in panicked haste, Æthelstan was not in control of the machine gun. With its stock folded back, he couldn't brace against the recoil, and his shots went wild, whanging and cracking all round the studio. Shockingly loud. Bond vaulted over a desk and hit the floor behind a sofa. It wouldn't give him any protection but at least he was hidden from Æthelstan and was no longer a clear target.

A bullet had torn through his leg, taking off a small chunk of flesh and ripping his pocket open. Its contents had spilled out. He snatched up what he could and threw himself in a long dive across the polished floor as the sofa erupted behind him in a shower of stuffing and splintered wood. The gun rattled one more time as he went into a roll and then righted himself next to one of the cameras, which were still tracking his every move.

Æthelstan was wrestling with the G36. It looked like he'd emptied the cartridge already. He flung the gun

ON HIS MAJESTY'S SECRET SERVICE

aside and ran to retrieve the fallen guard's weapon. Bond had ended up too far away to beat him to it and his leg felt weak and unreliable. He realised his hand was bleeding as well. Another bullet must have grazed it. He was clutching a handful of bloody coins, the largest of which was the fifty pence piece with the portrait of King Charles on it. He'd been carrying it since Heathrow.

Æthelstan had got to the gun. He was rising up, pulling back the spring-loaded charging handle. As he settled into position, Bond hurled the coin, flicking it with thumb and forefinger. It spun across the studio like a tiny ninja star and Bond's aim was lucky. The coin flew straight between Æthelstan's teeth, and he jerked his head back, coughed, choked, and spat it out.

It was all the edge Bond needed. Ignoring the screams of complaint from his wounded leg, he charged at Æthelstan and the two of them went down hard before Æthelstan could get a shot off.

Æthelstan shouted in pain as he landed, with Bond on top of him. A mercilessly hard slap round the face shut him up and made him compliant. Bond tore the gun out of his grip, thumbed the safety catch to single shot and got up, keeping the barrel trained on Æthelstan.

It was carnage in the studio. One of the cameras had been smashed into scrap by Æthelstan's chaotic gunplay and there was broken glass everywhere. It looked like he'd killed Canner, too. The South African lay on his back, unmoving, his body a bloody tatter, puncture holes across his chest and face. Bond went over and pulled off his lanyard with the plastic security badge attached, and, watching Æthelstan all the while, stuffed it in his pocket.

Ragnheiður was coming round. She got onto all fours, buckled and threw up.

'You all right?' Bond asked and she looked at him groggily.

'Never better.'

Her eyes were unfocused, but she was struggling to get a grip and managed to stand.

'Did I miss the party?'

'It's not over yet.'

Ragnheiður was still holding Canner's knife in a white-knuckle grip as she looked around the studio. Bond wondered if she'd ever been this close to death before. There was still so much he didn't know about her.

'I'm sorry,' he said. 'As a first date this is pretty appalling.'

Æthelstan looked up at them. 'Bond was right, Ragnheiður,' he said. 'You're a conniving little bitch.'

Ragnheiður squatted down next to him and pressed the blade to his eye. 'Watch what you say, Æthelstan – I'm a conniving little bitch with a knife.'

Bond gestured at Æthelstan with his gun. 'Get up.'

'You may have set my plans back, Bond,' said Æthelstan, struggling stiffly to his feet. 'But you've not stopped me, and you've not saved Charles.'

'I'm not in the mood for another one of your speeches, old man,' said Bond. 'Move it.'

They left the studio, Bond shepherding Æthelstan with the gun. Out in the tunnel, only the red emergency lights were lit, washing the stone walls in a sanguine glow. Ragnheiður used her ID badge to get them through the security doors and into a service lift.

'This will take us up to the kitchens,' she said. 'It's the quickest way out.'

The kitchens were empty at this time of night. And, so far, they'd seen none of Æthelstan's security guards. Bond hoped they'd been sent down to deal with the trouble that had blown up in camp, dead on four o'clock. But when they emerged from the kitchens into the main part of the castle, an alarm was blaring, and as they approached the entrance hall, they were aware of people and movement.

'We're going to have to front this out,' Bond said to Ragnheiður. 'Keep close to Æthelstan and keep that damn knife in his back. If he tries anything, kill him.'

There was chaos and confusion in the entrance hall. Three guards were arguing by the doors. They looked utterly clueless as to what was happening. A fourth guard, manning the desk, was involved in a shouting match with John Tyler and a group of Brits.

'It's all kicking off, Jonjo,' Tyler was yelling at the man. He was half dressed in t-shirt, shorts and trainers without socks. 'We're under attack. You have to give me my gun! It's back there in one of them boxes.'

There was a shout and Bond looked over to see Caiboche coming down the stairs with two other Frenchmen. They looked angry and fired up.

Bond made a snap decision. In times of chaos and uncertainty people always responded to the voice of authority.

'It's a set-up, Tyler,' he shouted. 'The French have sold us out. They're trying to get to Æthelstan.'

'I bloody knew it!'

'Don't trust his guards, either! It's a coup.'

This was all the encouragement John Tyler needed. He and the other Brits swarmed over the counter, overpowering the guard and grabbing his handgun. The other three guards turned and saw Æthelstan with Bond but weren't sure what this meant, or what they were supposed to do. In a moment, John Tyler was firing on Caiboche and the Frenchmen, who were diving for cover. The other Brits now emerged from behind the desk to take on the guards, armed with whatever they'd been able to get their hands on – one had a heavy torch, another was swinging a security metal detector, and a third must have found a G36 behind the counter because he was preparing to fire.

With the French keeping under cover and the guards preoccupied, Bond kept low and led Ragnheiður and Æthelstan past the X-ray machine and round behind the desk, where John Tyler and the guy with the G36 were keeping up a steady, but inaccurate, rate of fire.

Ragnheiður was still a little woozy. Bond told her to watch over Æthelstan and stay down, where they'd be protected by the solid marble desk. He then bundled into the side room with the stacked shelves of plastic boxes.

He needed his phone to connect with his back up, and the less evidence he could leave here, the better. He also wanted a better weapon for close-up work than the G36 slung over his back. The boxes were neatly labelled, and he soon found the name: Sanbourne. Peter. He pulled out the box, tore off the lid and retrieved his phone and the Glock.

By the time he emerged from the side room, everything had changed. John Tyler had been shot and was slumped on the floor, his dead eyes staring into the void. The other Brits were engaged in a hand-to-hand fight with Caiboche and his men. One of the guards was still standing. Still confused. Blocking the doors. Waiting for orders that would never come.

And Æthelstan was gone.

Bond swore.

Ragnheiður was sitting, leaning heavily on one arm. Her face white. She'd been sick again, and there was a nasty pool of mucous and bile on the floor. She looked up at Bond with a desolate expression.

'I'm sorry,' she muttered. 'I blacked out again. Æthelstan got away.'

'I can't let him escape,' said Bond. 'You'd better stay here.'

'No. I'm coming with you.'

Bond didn't have the time or the energy to argue with her.

'All right,' he said. 'But if you slow me down, I'll have to ditch you.'

'I won't.'

There was a shelf of plastic water bottles under the countertop. Bond tore the cap off one and gave it to Ragnheiður.

'Drink as much as you can.'

As she drank, he took stock of their position.

No sign of Æthelstan. He was the one man here nobody wanted to kill. Had he gone outside? To escape the carnage? If he had any sense he'd try to get as far away from the castle as possible.

Whatever the case, Bond's best bet was to get out of the hall. It'd be safer in the open, and he had to link up with Captain Cornwell and his men.

He squatted down and took hold of Ragnheiður by her shoulders.

'Ready?'

She nodded.

He offered her the Glock. 'You know how to use one of these?'

Another nod. 'Canner gave me training on the range.'

He gave her the gun. 'Let's go.'

He scrambled over the countertop, helped Ragnheiður, and then headed for the doors.

The guard moved to stop him and Bond had no alternative. The G36 spat three times, and the man went down. Bond was through the doors and out into the cold, wet night. Ragnheiður was wide-eyed in shock, but she kept up with him.

Bond tensed as a group of men and vehicles came storming up the driveway.

He relaxed.

'Thank God.'

It was Captain Cornwell and his men, most of them clinging onto five overloaded Polaris vehicles. From the bottom of the hill, Bond could hear the snap and crackle of gunfire and the occasional thump of an explosion.

Cornwell saw Bond and raised his eyebrows. His

cheek was scorched and there were patches of blood on his combat gear.

'Went off crazier than we could have imagined, sir,' he said, his voice husky and worn out. 'It's sodding Armageddon down there.'

'Any men lost?'

'Three walking wounded, but we're all still standing. We blew the substation at four as planned, got things started and left them to it.'

'Good man.' Bond dragged Lyle's lanyard and pass from his pocket and thrust it into Cornwell's hands, telling Ragnheiður to do the same. As she handed over her ID, Bond gave Cornwell his orders.

'Push through the entrance hall. Put down whoever you need. You have to get to the lowest floor. Use the service lift in the kitchens. Once you're down there, find Æthelstan's mainframes. Destroy everything. Blow the bloody doors off the whole bloody lot of it. I'm sure there's a more elegant way of doing things, but we don't have time for that. Anyone tries to get in your way – that's enemy action. But the guys working at the terminals, let them go. They won't put up a fight. Blow and go. The exit strategy remains the same. Over the border into Slovakia.'

'Understood.'

'And, Cornwell? On the way up here – did you pass another vehicle?'

'A big Jeep Defender going like a rat with its arse on fire.'

'That's our man.' Bond nodded to a nearby Polaris. 'How fast will these things go?'

'They're not exactly built for Formula One. Officially

50, but if you push it, you should do better than that. Off-road they're unbeatable. On the road . . . well. You'll feel like a Sunday driver. Keys in the ignition.'

Bond leapt into the vehicle, tossing the G36 onto the back seat. Ragnheiður joined him, climbing in the other side. She was still settling into her seat when Bond slammed the Polaris into low gear and set off.

'Get your seat belt on,' he said. 'I'm not going to be following the highway code.'

Bond pictured the driveway, snaking up the hillside in a series of gentle curves. If he was to have any hope of catching Æthelstan, he was going to have to cut a few corners. Literally.

He raced down to the security gates. They were hanging off their hinges and the bodies of the two guards were lying by the side of the road. Far below, Bond could see a car, almost at the bottom of the hill.

'Here goes.' Bond chose a straight line, directly down the hillside. Ragnheiður couldn't suppress a gasp as they left the road and crashed through a patch of low growing shrubs and then ploughed on through the soft, rain-sodden earth. The Polaris was wide enough to stay stable and had independent suspension and good ground clearance, but at this speed, and at so steep an angle, if Bond wasn't able to hold the vehicle to a straight line of descent it might easily flip over. He had to hold his nerve as it jostled and bounced and whined in complaint. He gripped the steering wheel tight, like a man holding onto the horns of a mad bull, wrestling to keep it in line.

They hit each section of road as they crossed it with

a bang and then launched off the other side so that they were airborne for a few seconds before slamming down onto the uneven ground.

The Polaris had no windscreen. It was just the bare bones of a vehicle, stripped down to nothing, with a roll bar instead of a roof. The rain had picked up and was spraying into their faces, so that Bond was soon drenched.

'Keep an eye on Æthelstan,' he shouted over the cacophony of the engine noise, the rushing wind and the undergrowth whipping at the bottom of the Polaris.

'He's out of the driveway and onto the road,' Ragnheiður shouted back.

'Damn. If only this thing would go faster.'

They scrambled over some rocks, the Polaris in its element, each wheel moving independently and gripping onto the boulders like the sure foot of a gecko. Past the rocks was a stretch of bare earth and then, at last, they were down and they slithered and skidded onto the road.

'You're bleeding,' said Ragnheiður, looking down at Bond's thigh. His seat was slick with blood. The Polaris was left hand drive and automatic and there was no clutch, so Bond could at least rest the leg.

'Can you strap it up for me?' he asked, and without replying, Ragnheiður started cutting off the long sleeve of her dress with Canner's knife.

As Bond concentrated on driving, Ragnheiður got the strip of cloth around his thigh and tied it fast. When she was done, he shouted to her to take the wheel.

She did as she was told, and Bond slipped his phone out of his pocket.

'Keep her in the middle of the road.'

A quick flurry of taps and swipes and he'd got the map on screen. It took no time to show their location. Another couple of taps and it showed other moving vehicles in the vicinity.

And there was Æthelstan in the Defender.

It only took Bond a moment to decide on a plan of action. The road swooped round in a long curve and then entered a forest where it followed a twisting path through the trees. They'd have to cut the corner and go directly cross-country. He'd got the hang of the Polaris and was enjoying its rugged, lightweight, off-road build and extraordinary stability. He knew it would cope.

He passed the phone to Ragnheiður and took control of the wheel again.

'That red dot's our man,' he said. 'We've got to get as close as we can to him. You're in charge. Waze isn't going to recommend the route we're going to take. You holding up?'

'I feel sick. My head hurts like the devil. And I can't see straight. But otherwise, I'm just fine.'

'Good for you.'

So saying, Bond steered the Polaris off the tarmac and they were once again slamming across the uneven ground. One moment they were scything through shrubbery, the next they were rumbling over rocks, tossing from side to side, and then they were splashing through boggy ground, but the Polaris ate it all up without a problem, never losing its grip. The headlight beam ahead of them danced and flickered, scribbling a crazy pattern over the darkness. Bond kept a firm hold on the wheel, his teeth clenched, blinking through spray and debris.

'You're doing it,' said Ragnheiður with an excited laugh. 'We're getting nearer.'

While Bond had closed the gap, he saw that there was no way he could get ahead of the Defender before they hit the forest.

As it was, though, they flew up a bank, and landed with a bone-shaking crunch only a few metres behind Æthelstan, his rear lights like the red eyes of some demonic animal.

Bond had to hope that Æthelstan wasn't used to driving himself. He probably had his own dedicated chauffeur, and wouldn't have the confidence to push the Defender at full speed through the switchbacks that snaked through the forest. As Bond pressured him, Æthelstan fishtailed around a corner, momentarily losing control, and after that, he dropped his speed considerably. Bond, by far the better driver, crept closer and closer, pushing the Polaris to its absolute limit.

Second by second, they gained on the Defender, its exhaust fumes threatening to choke them.

'Time to finish this,' Bond shouted. 'Use the Glock. Aim at his wheels and just keep pulling that trigger until you hit something. Okay?'

'Okay.'

Ragnheiður gritted her teeth, leaning forward and laying her gun arm flat on the body of the car. And then she started firing. *Bam-bam-bam-bam-bam*, like someone hammering a nail into a piece of wood. The outcome was disappointing. The Glock had been emptied and the Defender seemed unharmed.

'I'm sorry.'

'Save it.'

Bond knew how hard it was to hit a car at speed when you were firing from another moving vehicle. Any tiny jolt of your hand was translated into the shot going metres wide. And Æthelstan was growing more confident, speeding up, slewing round the bends.

'Use the G36,' Bond yelled. 'It'll be even more inaccurate, but if you set it to automatic, you'll spray him with bullets. We just have to hope that one finds its mark.'

Ragnheiður got the G36 from the back, unfolded the stock and fiddled with the firing control until she was ready.

The gun gave a drum roll, another and another . . .

It looked like nothing was going to happen. And then Æthelstan's car gave a shudder and was suddenly spinning round. Æthelstan tried to right it, and over-steered in the opposite direction. The Defender twisted, tipped over, rolled and left the road, smashing through some saplings and disappearing into the forest.

Bond pressed down hard on the brake pedal and the Polaris skidded and slid to a halt. Ragnheiður was out before him. She ran back along the road and into the trees where the Defender lay on its top, clinking and ticking as it cooled. Steam rising with a hiss. One back wheel still spinning pathetically.

Bond was hard on Ragnheiður's heels and before he could stop her, she'd emptied the rest of the cartridge into the car, not caring what she hit.

'That's enough,' Bond said gently. 'It's over.'

Ragnheiður dropped the gun. She was weeping. Going into shock. Bond pushed past her and went to the Defender. Æthelstan was still alive. His door had come open in the accident and he was crawling out. His face a red mask, his nose flattened, one eyebrow hanging off.

Bond pulled him clear.

Defiant to the end, Æthelstan laughed, spitting blood from between his teeth.

'Too little, too late, Bond,' he grunted. 'My birthday's coming soon, and I'm going to have my party. It'll be a history lesson for everyone. Everybody will remember me, and they will remember the birth of Alfred the Great. We'll be forever united in history.'

'You should know, Æthelstan, that history is written by the winners. And you're on the losing side here.'

Bond checked the man for damage. All the while thinking about the damage Æthelstan had caused to others – and the carnage he'd been hoping to unleash. He thought about 009 and Moneypenny. He thought about M. He thought about how men like Æthelstan often became stronger if they were caught and imprisoned. Becoming martyrs to their cause.

'You've a bullet in your chest,' he said. 'If it's not seen to fast, you'll likely die.'

'Well, come on, then,' Æthelstan said bitterly. 'Aren't you going to call for an ambulance? You're not going to leave me lying here, I hope. We're both Englishmen, after all.'

'Not me,' said Bond. 'Half-Scottish, half-Swiss.'

'Shit . . . I knew I couldn't trust you.'

Bond held Æthelstan's head gently between his hands. He looked away, and then gave a quick twist. Felt Æthelstan's neck snap.

Ragnheiður was sitting on a stump, exhausted. Bond hauled her up.

'It's time we were out of here,' he said.

She looked at him bleakly.

'Who are you?' she said.

'Just another foot soldier following orders.'

She softened, put her arms around him and hugged him tight.

May 4th – 2 days to
the Coronation

Bond looked at his watch. 8.35. He had 13 minutes.

The mission now was to avoid any hint of scandal. Any interruption to the smooth progress of the coronation. The public mustn't be spooked. The media mustn't be spooked. The markets mustn't be spooked. And the royal family mustn't be spooked.

The illusion of a calm, stately succession must be kept up.

In the end, all MI6 had was a theory – that there was still a viable threat to Charles. It was an incomplete theory, and, without anything else to go on, the only way to conclusively prove it and ensure that there wouldn't be a future threat to the king, was to let the plot unfold.

Which wasn't an option.

In the end, it might all add up to nothing. It might just be an empty threat from a cornered and desperate Æthelstan, wanting to have the last word. He'd hinted at something. But what? Neither Bond, nor anybody else at MI6 had managed to get to the heart of it. It had been Ragnheiður who had unravelled the first clue. Lying beside Bond in a hotel in Vienna, her skin warm against his.

Getting out of Hungary had been mercifully straight-forward. Their pickup had been waiting in the vicinity, tracking Bond's phone as soon as he'd retrieved it and switched it on. Less than 10 minutes after Æthelstan's car had left the road an ambulance had arrived, manned by MI6 operatives. They'd taken Bond and Ragnheiður on board and patched Bond up. As Hungary and Slovakia are both part of the Schengen Area there were no border checks and no need to show documents, so, half an hour later they were across the border into Slovakia, where Bond was informed that Cornwell's men, having successfully completed their mission, had been exfiltrated on a coach posing as an athletics team.

On receiving the news, Bond, utterly exhausted and flushed with relief, had fallen into a deep sleep, and floated into Austria in the arms of Morpheus, safely strapped to a stretcher in the back of the ambulance.

He'd been debriefed in the embassy on Jaurèsgasse, while Ragnheiður had survived a grilling from staff in another room.

Once he'd told them all he could, Bond had been awarded the luxury of one night in a discreet boutique hotel. He'd taken a small suite that was filled with all the food and drink and luxuries he'd need to be able to lock the door and stay there for 24 hours without leaving.

Before switching on the 'do not disturb' sign and locking the door, he'd let Ragnheiður in. They'd kissed, drawn the curtains, lit a candle and then shared a bath in a giant, claw-footed, free-standing tub. Luxuriating in the healing heat, Ragnheiður had been fascinated by the tracery of scars across Bond's body. Asking him to tell her the story behind every one.

They then slipped between the cool, crisp cotton sheets of their king-sized bed and it was Bond's turn to examine her body, paying close attention to every part of it.

They were safe at last here. In a world of their own. Bond shut out everything else. They had shared an extraordinary adventure, and both had stared into the face of death. Ragnheiður was the only person who knew what Bond had been through, and the only person who would understand. He couldn't give himself to anyone else at this moment. And for her part, Bond was the only person who could understand what Ragnheiður had been through.

There were tensions they both needed to relieve, there were emotions they both needed to share, and they both desperately sought a physical release. A letting go that can only happen in that moment of mutual ecstasy.

Yasmin wouldn't understand and Bond could never tell her anything of what had happened in Hungary. This part of his life was shut off to her.

Afterwards, satiated and drowsy, drunk on pleasure, they lay there, skin on skin, and stared into each other's eyes.

'Do you really think I'm a lying little bitch?' Ragnheiður asked him, with a smile.

'I'm sorry. You know I had to convince them that you'd really betrayed me.'

'Even when we lie, we tell the truth.'

'Perhaps. It's the problem in our game,' said Bond. 'We all wear masks, pretend we're something we're not, and to make that work, we have to believe it ourselves. We risk losing track of who we really are, and who, in the end, we're deceiving. In the castle, inside that studio, I had to wonder – were you playing a double cross? A triple cross? Until you cut the ties, I had no way of knowing.'

'So, did a part of you think that I had really betrayed you? That I wasn't going to help you? Did a part of you really think of me as a bitch?'

'No,' said Bond and he kissed her. 'Whatever the truth. Whoever's side you were on. I was in awe of you. I still am. You're a supernatural creature.'

'I'm just a woman. Why do men always have to turn us into something else? Into goddesses, Madonnas, muses, nymphs?'

'Because we can never really know you.'

'You think I might still be bluffing now? Trying to work my way into the heart of MI6?'

'I don't want to think about anything anymore. Can't we just lie here and enjoy this moment?'

'No,' said Ragnheiður. 'First you have to make love to me one more time.'

'You'll have to wait,' Bond said and laughed. 'I'm

151

not Superman. First, I need a good meal, a nice fat steak, some green vegetables full of iron, some decent wine, a glass of brandy . . .'

'Bah.'

'There's no rush, darling. We've got all night.'

Ragnheiður propped herself up on an elbow, and stared at him.

'It was a big risk, James. Are you always so reckless? You put yourself in terrible danger. Letting them catch you.'

Bond sighed. 'You know I had no choice. I had to get into the heart of Æthelstan's operation, see it for myself. I had to be standing right next to him at 4 o'clock when Cornwell blew the substation. I couldn't risk him saving the day or getting away. And I had to know that if we shut down the operations in the castle, we were shutting down his *whole* operation.'

'And *did* you shut the whole thing down?'

Bond silenced her with a kiss.

'I said I didn't want to talk about all this, now.'

'But you have to. Is it over?'

Bond got up and went to fetch a bottle of Jameson's from the little kitchen area. Poured himself a glass. Sank it.

'No,' he said, bluntly. 'It's not over. What haunts me is that Æthelstan was so insistent that he had a backup plan. He gave hints. You know how he loved to talk. Loved to taunt us with how clever he thought he was. He was so desperate to tell us what his ingenious plan was . . . but always stopped himself just in time.'

'Operation Æthelflæd,' said Ragnheiður.

'Exactly,' said Bond. 'What is it?'

'Pour me one of those,' she replied.

Bond brought a second glass of whisky over to the bed, and Ragnheiður sat up, wrapped in the sheet. Deep in thought.

'I don't know what it all means,' said Bond, running his fingers through his hair. 'And it makes me feel stupid. What's the significance of his birthday? May the 4th? Is something going to happen? Is that his backup plan? And Operation 848? Why was he so sure that Alfred's birth date and his would be forever remembered together? Why would you remember 848 on May the 4th?'

'It's a time,' said Ragnheiður, her eyes bright.

'What do you mean, "a time"?'

'8:48. It's the time on the 4th that his back-up plan kicks in.'

'Dear God, I think you could be right. You're amazing. So what about Operation Æthelflæd . . .'

'Æthelflæd was King Alfred's daughter. Yes?'

'Yes. Æthelstan banged on about her continuing what Alfred had started. Uniting the country. Defeating his enemies. But Æthelstan and Marina have no children. That's a dead end.'

And it was still a dead end. Bond and M and all the big minds at MI6 hadn't got any further than a possible date, and a possible time. It was all very tenuous. Not enough to call the coronation off. Not enough to keep Charles locked up out of sight until the potential danger had passed. Not enough to cause ripples.

After lengthy discussions with Palace security, it had been decided that they couldn't simply cancel everything Charles had to do before the coronation. Every minute of every day in a monarch's life was accounted for, arranged months, often years, in advance. Things could sometimes be changed at the last minute, like the recent cancellation of his planned meeting with Macron in France, to avoid Charles getting caught up in the strikes and civil unrest that were raging there after Macron's attempts to raise the pension age from 62 to 64. But the coronation could not be cancelled. It had to proceed with no outward signs of panic and uncertainty.

And today's rehearsal was also set in stone. Nothing could be changed at this late stage.

Instead, Charles had been surrounded with extra security. Two of his entourage were MI5 agents, Kingsley and Isaacson. There were extra agents, police and military around the Abbey. Charles's bodyguards had been briefed, but he himself had been kept in the dark.

Bond had insisted that not all of their intelligence was shared with Charles's team. The services had no idea who they could trust. And whilst the royal entourage knew there was an extra, and very secret, security operation in progress, the details and all of the personnel involved had not been fully disclosed.

The plan was that at 8:40 Charles would be taken to a safe space, under the pretext of signing some documents and a photo-op. He'd be kept there until 9.15, when, if it was all clear, he'd be let out to carry on with his duties.

The safe space was not ideal, but it was the best they could improvise under pressure of time. Sixteen metres above the Abbey floor, accessed by a newly built tower, were the Queen's Jubilee Galleries. Various treasures from the building were displayed here, and one section was devoted to its royal history of coronations, weddings and funerals.

The Galleries might not have been perfect, but there was still much to recommend them as a safe space. They were small enough to be contained, and had been easy to secure. The area was 'sterile' – wooden floors, bare brick walls, no hiding places. And there was only one way in or out – via the lift, or stairs, inside the access tower.

The plan was that Charles would be taken up to sign some official documents at a table that had been installed in front of a huge portrait of his mother, Queen Elizabeth. Bulletproof screens had been erected on either side so that Charles was protected from any potential exterior threat.

The security team had been over every square centimetre of the galleries, removing anything that could be used as a weapon and checking for bugs and hidden electronic devices. They'd dismantled the light fitting and plug sockets. They'd crawled around on their hands and knees, mounted stepladders, checked inside every cabinet. They'd taken the desk apart and examined the chair.

The area was indeed 'sterile'. Safe. Secure.

Both the cameramen filming the signing and the

photographer were also MI5 men, but even so, the cameras had been studied in microscopic detail before being allowed into the galleries and set up.

It was now 8:38, and there was nothing more Bond could do.

He saw that Charles and his team were starting to make their apologies, ready for his departure. The girl with the French braid and the brisk, head-girl manner was gesturing for the King to move on, all smiles.

Bond felt his phone vibrate. He fished it out and woke it up.

To the Tweed Suit next to him, this was the ultimate outrage. Particularly as he, and everyone else, had been asked to surrender their phones to security as they came into the building.

Bond winked at the man and walked quickly away ahead of the royal party down the South Ambulatory towards the entrance to Weston Tower. He checked the caller ID – Ragnheiður.

Bond had set the phone to its highest level of security. All incoming calls went via Regent's Park. The team there vetted them and must have patched her through. Which meant this was important.

He accepted the call and put the phone to his ear. Said one word.

'Bond.'

'He had a daughter.' Ragnheiður sounded serious. Urgent.

'What?' Bond was waved through the tower entrance by the two soldiers standing guard.

'I used my people,' said Ragnheiður. 'The underground network. There's a lot of deep radicals out there who partied when Æthelstan died. They've been tracing back through all of his life. Digging up dirt. Finding out anything they could about him.'

Bond stood off to one side as Charles and his team arrived. The lift shaft formed the core of the tower. Wooden stairs climbing up around it.

'Be quick,' Bond hissed. 'It's nearly 8:48.'

The girl in the French braid spotted him on his phone and frowned. Charles was chatting to one of his close team as they got into the lift. The two MI5 officers followed them in with the girl. Bond couldn't join them while he was still on the phone. And, even if he did, he risked losing his signal.

He started up the stairs, his phone clamped to his ear. Fully aware that it was a seven storey climb to the galleries. Ragnheiður's voice sounded very close and a thousand miles away at the same time.

'When Æthelstan was a student in the 80s, at somewhere called de Montfort University, he was sleeping with three other students. One of them, Ann Hayes, got pregnant. He tried to get her to have an abortion, but she refused and kept the child. A daughter. Æthelstan secretly paid her support.'

Bond was leaping up the stairs, four at a time, keeping a hard, steady pace.

'Do you have a name?' Already it hurt to talk.

'She grew up as Christina Hayes. I gave her name to your team.'

'I always said you were a wonder, Ragnheiður.'

There was the beep of another call coming in. Bond checked the screen. It was Louis Gaughan from the communications team at Regent's Park. Without a word, he cut Ragnheiður off and accepted the call.

'Did you speak to Ragnheiður, Bond?'

'Yes.' Bond grunted.

'Seems she was right,' said Finney. 'We tracked down Christina Hayes. She changed her name to Flora Woodbridge in the late 90s.'

Bond turned a corner. Headed up the next flight. The outer wall of the tower was mostly glass and alternate views of the Houses of Parliament and the bulk of the Abbey spun past him as he circled upwards.

'Go on.'

'High-flying career in the city, then charity work, then the Royal household. I'm sending you a photograph.'

'Save it,' Bond snapped. He was fighting for breath. Lactic acid burning in his lungs. Spitting out the words between breaths as his feet pounded up the wooden steps. 'Know what she looks like . . .' He sucked in more air. 'French braid.'

Bond killed the call.

Still clutching the phone, he forced himself to put on more speed, no matter how much it hurt. He was gasping. His breath hoarse. His legs rapidly turning to jelly.

Another flight, another corner, and then, *thank God*, he was there. He'd reached the top. He stuffed his phone back in his pocket and pushed on through to the galleries.

He saw that Charles and his party had paused to talk to the photographer. A pre-arranged delaying tactic in case Bond wasn't able to arrive at the same time as Charles.

Good. He paused for a moment to regain his composure. Doubled over. He took in a great lungful of oxygen, exhaled slowly and felt his heart rate drop, then straightened up and nodded to the photographer.

Charles's group moved on towards the screened off area, the two MI5 men bringing up the rear. Bond wiped the sweat from his face and walked up behind Flora Woodbridge. He took hold of her elbow. She turned, surprised. Bond smiled.

'Can I borrow you for a moment, Miss Woodbridge?'

'What? What do you mean? I have no idea who you are.'

Bond nodded to the MI5 agents. Isaacson continued towards the screened-off area with Charles and his entourage; the other, Kingsley, held back.

'This won't take long,' said Bond, keeping polite, neutral. 'I just need to ask you a few questions.'

'I can't do that now.' Flora looked affronted. 'This is ridiculous. I have His Majesty's pen. He'll need me.'

As she spoke, she dug a fat fountain pen out of her handbag and waved it in Bond's face as if she was worried that a commoner like him might not know what a such a thing was.

'That can wait,' said Bond. And, still holding her elbow, he began to lead her away towards Weston Tower.

'No. It can't wait.' Flora was getting flustered, and

her cut-glass accent was cracking. She struggled to free herself from Bond's grip. 'His Majesty is very particular about what pen he uses.'

'I'm sure he is. He'll just have to use a biro this time. Come with me.' Bond's voice had turned cold and hard. Before Flora could say anything else, he raised an eyebrow to Kingsley who took hold of her other arm. They walked her out of the galleries and stopped at the lift. Kingsley let Flora go and secured the heavy doors behind them. Sealing the three of them off from the galleries.

Flora was still protesting.

'Save it,' said Bond with no sympathy in his voice. 'I know who you are, so you can stop this charade. You're Æthelstan's daughter. His reincarnation of Æthelflæd. And I know that you were intending to harm the King in some way, at precisely 8:48.'

'Are you mad? That's just about the most preposterous thing I've ever heard.'

'Believe me. I'd be very happy to be proved wrong,' said Bond. 'But whatever happens, you're going to be taken from here and incarcerated in the depths of MI5 until they get to the truth. What's the time, Kingsley?'

'8:47.'

At this, Flora changed, turning suddenly into a cornered cat, showing her teeth and spitting. She whipped the lid off the pen and swiped it at Bond. His gut reaction kicked in and he ducked out of the way just in time. And now he knew what the plan was.

'Keep away from the pen!' he shouted at Kingsley.

Too late. Kingsley was already on the move, trying to pin Flora against the windows of the staircase, and she was just able to scratch the nib down his cheek, leaving a trail of inky black liquid. Kingsley swore and got his hands to her wrists. And then he grimaced. Twitched. Shook his head. He let go of her as his lips curled back from teeth that were clamped together. The sinews were standing out in his neck like steel cables. He groaned and his back arched grotesquely, as if he might break in two, and finally he collapsed backwards and tumbled down the stairs.

Flora turned on Bond, grinning in triumph, holding the pen like a dagger.

Bond had wondered who would be crazy enough to attempt to assassinate Charles face to face in the midst of heavy security. Well, here was his answer. Flora appeared to be totally unhinged. What lies had Æthelstan fed to her? How would he have worked on her? Turned her into this spitting, hissing, carrier of death?

He backed away towards the top of the stairs as she advanced on him. God knows what the poison was in that pen. It had to be some kind of fast-acting nerve agent. Lethal enough to kill Charles before any antidote could be delivered. Poor Kingsley was probably already dead.

Bond was gripped by a terrible rage. He wanted to lash out at her, tear her heart out. He wanted to utterly annihilate her, just as she'd so heedlessly killed Kingsley, and had been planning to do to Charles. The rage welled up inside him like rising bile, and then, just as quickly as it had come upon him, it ebbed away, leaving him with a dull, numb, emptiness.

This was a pathetic scene. A grubby little fight outside a lift. And yet it somehow embodied all the hate in the world, all the needless destruction, all the hurt that men do.

It was time to stop Flora.

Black poison dripped from the pen nib as she slashed it at him, writing a giant X in the air between them.

'Give it up, Flora,' he said. 'This is over. The time's passed.'

She must have been planning this attack for months, working out the details, practising. But Bond had been training all his life for moments such as this. He just had to think of the pen as a knife and let his muscle memory come in to play.

He dodged round to the stairs and started to back down them. He had the advantage here. Flora would have to lean down to stab at him. Off balance. He faked a stumble, and she surged towards him with a cry of triumph, the pen held out in front of her.

He grabbed her forearm and pulled it towards him, using Flora's own momentum to carry her past him so that she flew headfirst down the stairs, landing with a sickening crunch next to Kingsley on the landing where the stairs turned a corner.

The pen had flown out of her grip and hit the windows, spraying its toxic black load over the glass. It fell onto a step, somehow both innocuous and lethal at the same time. Bond skipped over it, pulling his cuffs from his pocket as he went. In a moment he'd got to Flora, lifted one of her wrists and locked it to the banister.

She gave out a long, deep, inhuman groan, like a sick cow, and lay there, shuddering. A figure appeared at the top of the stairs. It was the second MI5 man, Isaacson. He quickly took in the situation.

'See to Kingsley.' Bond headed back up the stairs. 'He's been poisoned. We need a service ambulance ASAP. Call up the cleaning crew. And, whatever you do, don't touch this black gunk on the glass or that pen lying there.'

Bond tossed Isaacson the key for the cuff as he hurried past him and headed into the galleries. One of Charles's bodyguards was waiting on the other side of the doors.

Bond looked him in the eyes, searching for any signs of worry. He said one word. 'Charles?'

'No problem,' said the bodyguard dispassionately. 'Apart from having to improvise with a pen to sign the documents, 8.48 passed without a hitch. False alarm, I guess.'

'Yeah . . . I guess. Keep these doors shut, though, and don't come out until the agreed time.'

'No problem.' Bond detected the hint of a smirk. As far as the bodyguard was concerned, this was just MI6 playing silly buggers.

Bond returned to the stairs, pulling the doors closed behind him. In less than a minute the lift arrived and four people wearing hazmat suits stepped out. Covered from head to toe in shiny yellow coveralls, gloves, boots and gas masks, there was no way of telling whether they were men or women. Between them they carried a serious amount of clean-up equipment. Bond explained the situation and watched as they went to work. Two of them set about collecting as much of the poison as they could, a third scoured the stairs for any other hazardous material, while the fourth collected and bagged the pen.

Bond looked at his watch. They had twelve minutes to remove any trace of the attack.

The lift pinged again, signalling the arrival of the emergency medical team.

'Sedate the woman. Get our man down as quickly as possible.'

The new crew went to work, fast and efficient, and Bond felt a wave of nausea and tiredness come over him. He went to the window and looked across at the Palace of Westminster. The black statue of King Richard I astride his charger on the lawn. One arm raised to the heavens, his war sword pointing straight up. Like some kind of mounted superhero.

There would never be any statues erected to Bond. His dirty work must forever remain secret. Besides, what heroic pose would they put him in? Breaking a man's neck? Scuffling in a stairwell? Cuffing an injured woman to a handrail? But then, Richard the Lionheart hadn't exactly had a hero's death. Shot by a teenager with a crossbow. Died of gangrene.

Bond shook his head, rolled his shoulders, dispelling the dark thoughts, then went back to supervising the clean-up. By 9:15 there was no evidence that anything had ever taken place here and Bond was standing quietly, waiting, hands clasped at his waist, neat and anonymous.

There was a click and a rattle and Charles came through the doors with his entourage, midway through a sentence.

'signing endless bloody bits of paper, posing for photographs nobody ever sees, that's the job of a modern monarch.'

He and his equerries laughed. Bond was less than a metre away from the King. Charles saw him, smiled and nodded politely as he went past. Safe and secure. Oblivious.

In a moment, the lift swallowed them up. The king would probably never know the part that Bond had played in saving his life, and that suited Bond. He didn't want a statue. Didn't want a damned knighthood. If he became a public figure, he'd have to quit the service, he'd be public property, would have to face a lot of questions.

And he didn't know what the answers were.

He took the 50 pence coin from his pocket. He noticed that there was a little crust of dried blood between the letters of Charles's name. He scraped it off with his thumb and put the coin away. He told himself that the next time a homeless person asked him for money he'd give them this coin with Charles's head on it.

No souvenirs.

He thought about what he'd said to Ragnheiður after he'd broken Æthelstan's neck. That he was just a soldier following orders. He'd almost choked on the words as he'd said them. He knew it was a standard way of absolving yourself from any responsibility, any guilt.

I did what I was told. Just doing my duty. Just following orders.

He worked for M, who ran the 00 department, part of MI6, and ultimately, he was in the service of His Majesty the King.

What if you're ordered to do something you know is wrong? Do you do as you're told, do your 'duty', or do you follow a moral code above and beyond that duty?

He hadn't killed Æthelstan in a fight. He hadn't done it to save himself, or anyone else. In that moment, nobody else was under threat. Bond had the opportunity to change history. Let Æthelstan live and he becomes a martyr, still spreading his poison, like the black liquid in Flora's pen. Or, in M's words, put him down like a mad dog before he bit anyone else?

In the end, it had been Bond's choice. He could only live by accepting responsibility for his own actions. He was his own man. With his own code.

He could quit the service any time he wanted. 00 agents usually left the service before they were retired. Each kill getting harder than the last. The toll mounting. The burden getting heavier. The agent crumbling.

Bond wasn't there, yet. He still had a few more years in him. Because when it came down to it, this was the only life he knew. Being on the move, living in hotels, eating in restaurants, wandering the globe, carrying a gun.

And, if necessary, pulling the trigger.

If he retired, what on earth would he do? Would he just turn into Peter Sanbourne? Become a security consultant? Get a desk job somewhere?

Working for the service had been the making of him but the ruin of him too. It had left him unfit to do anything else.

He looked at his reflection in the windows. Straightened his hair. Adjusted his tie. Ran his hands down his jacket, to ease out the wrinkles. He sniffed.

'Come on, old man,' he said. 'You need a drink.'

He smiled. Closed a door in his mind and locked it. No more introspection. It was time to lose himself for a while.

He took his phone out and called Ragnheiður back.

'You cut me off,' she said. 'Don't you love me anymore?'

'Oh, I'm madly in love with you Ragnheiður – whatever love means. But I have to warn you. I'm not the marrying kind.'

Ragnheiður made a dismissive noise.

'Don't worry, James. I'm not the marrying kind, either.'

END

An Interview with
Charlie Higson

Q: If someone had told you at the start of 2023 that within one year you would write and publish an original, best-selling, adult James Bond novel, what would you have said?

A: I'd have told them to **** off! It's not possible. There just isn't time. When Ian Fleming Publications (IFP) presented the idea to me, they said it would have to be a short story, because they only had a small amount of time to prepare it. They approached me in mid-February and wanted to publish the story at the beginning of May to coincide with the Coronation of King Charles III. And all they had was a title – On *His* Majesty's Secret Service. Perhaps, if I had an idea for a story, I might be able to get up to 10,000 words? Perhaps... Even coming up with a short story would be hard to pull off, but I thought the concept was fun. 2023 was the 70th anniversary of the publication of the first Bond book, *Casino Royale*. It also happened to be the 60th anniversary of the publication of *On Her Majesty's Secret Service*, doing a twist on it was a nice idea. It seemed that several things were nicely aligned – the anniversaries, the Coronation, the fact that the proceeds would go to charity, and I felt there was a general hunger among fans for a new Bond adventure. I thought that if I could come up with a good idea I could probably write it quite quickly. In the initial meeting IFP said it was probably best to avoid any kind of plot about trying to assassinate Charles or disrupt the Coronation. And I said, 'Come on, there isn't another plot. That's it.' They had to concede that it was a good idea. I was very pleased that in the end we did it with The National Literacy Trust, a charity that I do a lot of work with. The Queen is involved with it too, so it felt appropriate. Once I had that idea – a plot to disrupt the Coronation – it all came to me pretty quickly.

Q: Did the work you've done on your history podcast help the writing process at all?

A: That did help. It gave me the germ of the background. Fleming famously wrote about things he was interested in. He did a lot of research on diamond smuggling and wrote a book about it, for instance – *The Diamond Smugglers*, which obviously served as the base research for *Diamonds are Forever*. He loved skiing, scuba diving, swimming, international travel... and he put all these things into the books. When he got interested in genealogy, it fed into *On Her Majesty's Secret Service*.

I had plans to launch a podcast for the Coronation called *Willy Willy Harry Stee*, which is a history of the British monarchy in chronological order. I've always been interested in the idea that the monarchy is this stately progression from one King or Queen to another. It's not. It's a twisted tale of madness, anarchy and violence; these people are forever deposing each other, or killing each other and shoving red hot pokers up their fundaments. And there's a thread that runs through the royal story – *who has the right to sit on the throne?* When I was researching the podcast I came across a lot of slightly mad, far-right groups who are obsessed with 'Saxon Purity'. The idea that our rightful monarchs are not the Windsors. Even though the Anglo-Saxons are no more pure English than the Romans, the Vikings or the Normans.

I thought this would be a great background for my villain, who is tapping into the resentment there is in this country about people losing their essential Englishness and being swamped by foreign peoples and ideas – an anxiety and obsession that goes back at least to King Alfred the Great's time. Thinking up a new Bond villain, with some kind of new sinister plan, is tough, but I was pleased with Æthelstan of Wessex. He's created an unholy alliance to disrupt the Coronation and ostensibly put himself on the throne. He claims to be able to trace his line directly back to Alfred the Great and that Charles can't. But, in fact, everybody could trace their line back to Alfred the Great, if they had the patience. As it turns out, Æthelstan has a deeper, more devious plan than the one he's sold to his supporters.

Q: How did a 10,000 word short story turn into this 42,000 word novella?

A: I got carried away. Once I had the story worked out, I set about slotting in the classic elements of a Bond book. This is the great thing about Fleming: he very cleverly came up with a re-usable structure that saved him a huge amount of time and effort. A classic Bond story starts with M giving Bond a file, and essentially saying, 'This is the villain, this is what he's up to, go and sort him out.'

Now, in a normal spy book, finding out all that stuff might be the first three quarters of the story. You have to get to the heart of a mystery. But here M has already done it and Bond is just going to finish it off. We're coming in near the end. So, you can set up a story really quickly. Then you just have to slot in the other classic elements: Bond goes off and gets involved with the villain's organisation, he has some kind of confrontation early on – a game of golf, or cards, a skirmish with henchmen, whatever – which helps him get closer to the villain. He meets the henchmen, he meets the woman, he's captured, he's tortured, he escapes, and he turns the tables. He then kills the villain and destroys his organisation. Finally, Bond is allowed to spend some quality time with the woman. That's it. No twists and turns, just clean, strong storytelling with a mythical underpinning of good vs. evil. With M as the King, Bond as his knight errant and the villain as the dragon (if you want to extend the metaphor further, you can add in Major Boothroyd/Q as Merlin the magician giving the knight enchanted items to help in his quest... And the Walther PPK as Excalibur!)

So I had the villain and the villain's plot. Next was the location.

Bond is MI6, the international wing of the secret services, so his adventures have to be abroad. I'd just been to Hungary, a lovely country and one I was really fascinated with, so I decided to send Bond there.

Now I had all the elements in place and they were simple enough to work as a short story, but as I started writing it, I got carried away, because I had so much Bond in my head from a lifetime of watching films and reading books and writing books about Bond. It just came pouring out. I remember ringing up IFP and saying, 'Is it alright if it's a bit longer than 10,000 words?' And they said 'the longer the better – go for it'. And then, when I was just about to deliver, I got in touch and said, 'Can you wait another couple of days because I want to put in a car chase?' Before I knew it, we had over 40,000 words, about the same length as the shorter Fleming books.

Q: Did you look specifically at any of Ian Fleming's short stories when working on OHMSS?

A: Yes, I re-read all his short stories because I wanted to see how he managed to fit the essence of a classic Bond story into the format of a short story. Some of them were written as short stories originally and some of them were based on treatments for a James Bond TV series that he was planning but which never got made. It was interesting to see how you could get the essence of Bond, the villain, the girl, the violence, the glamorous foreign settings and the action into a short story. It was useful and encouraging, and it got Fleming's voice back into my head.

Q: Ian famously wrote at speed. He would write his books in less than three months. Were there any benefits to writing as fast as you did?

A: I think there were. It was good to just get on and do it. Not overthink it. Fleming famously used to say that he thought a big part of the success of his books was the fact that he had an adolescent mind. And I think he meant that he didn't have that adult standing over his shoulder saying, 'That's a bit far-fetched, Ian. I don't think you can do that. You wouldn't do that in a proper book.' But he was like, 'No, I want to do this, it'll be fun, it'll be exciting.' And I did the same thing. I thought, 'Why don't I just do what I want to do and not make it too big and complicated?' Fleming's books are mostly quite short and to the point. I had to stick to that so I couldn't go off on any discursive detours.

I just got my head down and wrote quickly – to a soundtrack of Bond film music blasting out of my computer speakers. All that energy came from 007. IFP approached me mid-February, I submitted an outline for the story which was approved by the end of February, I wrote it in March, we turned it around in April – editing, copy editing, proofreading, printing, and it was in the shops on May 4th, two days before the Coronation. Because I knew from the start what publication day would be, I could work that into the book, which begins on the day the book was published. It was great fun being able to play around with all this stuff.

Q: 2025 will mark 20 years since *Silverfin* came out, which means 20 years since you started working on Bond. Is the Bond in this new book the natural progression of your Young Bond? And is he your Bond or Ian's bond, if you see them in any way different?

A: When I was approached about doing Young Bond, the idea was to keep the timeline, as far as possible, linked in with Fleming's timeline. So, my Young Bond books are set in the early '30s, a great time in history to have fun adventures in.

I always thought that if I did an adult Bond, it would be a continuation of that timeline: the '40s, getting into the start of the Second World War, maybe showing how he becomes an agent and how he gets his 00 status. But, when the offer to write an adult Bond was made to me, I realised it would have to be contemporary, to tie in with the Coronation, and I had to throw out what I had planned for my adult Bond. What's interesting is that Bond is pretty much always 35 years old. Fleming kept him that age over the course of about 10 years, which means the backstory doesn't really add up. It's not consistent. If you follow Fleming's books, Bond bought his first Bentley when he was about 10 years old (which I did actually manage to work into my Young Bond book, *Double or Die*). Also, the Bond actors in the films are classically about 35 when they start. I thought, 'Okay. I've got to write about a 35-year-old man in 2023, which means he would have been born at the end of the 1980s,' whereas Fleming's Bond is a product of the Second World War. He was Fleming's portrayal of a new type of man, a new type of anti-hero, based on the sort of people he knew in the war, this new breed of agents and commandos. A lot of them were from posh backgrounds but were essentially violent psychopaths. They went through hell and turned into different people. That was Ian's idea for Bond, he wanted to show someone who has been damaged by his experiences in the Second World War and the evil he's witnessed, which leaves him with extreme views about 'nasty foreigners' and that kind of thing.

But a 35-year-old Englishman today hasn't been through all of that. They're living in a very different world and have been moulded by very different forces and events. My eldest son is 31, so only four or five years younger than the Bond that I'm writing. Young men today have different attitudes and a different view of the world. So, I had to make my Bond be believable as a contemporary 30-something man, but still be recognisably, at his core, Fleming's Bond – he's a loner, he's tough, he's resourceful, he's relentless.

Q: You finished writing Young Bond in 2009. Since then, we've had all of Daniel Craig's movies and many new adult Bond books. How has writing Bond changed in that time? Perhaps the world of Bond has changed?

A: Inevitably. What EON, who make the films, have done so cleverly is reinvent Bond for each new generation, whilst keeping him recognisably Bond. I mean, in many ways, Roger Moore's Bond and Sean Connery's Bond are completely different characters. In the '70s, when journalists asked Roger Moore how seriously he was going to take this character, he said, 'This is a so-called secret agent who could walk into any bar in the world and the barman's going to say, "Ah, Mr Bond, I've made you a martini, shaken not stirred!" I'm not going to take him seriously at all.' He said it was ridiculous and so he was going to have fun with it. It reflected the times of the '70s. Timothy Dalton reflected the changes to society in the '80s – the era when we had the birth of Political Correctness and the acceptance of women's liberation and feminism. Pierce Brosnan was the embodiment of the '90s, brash, designer, lads' mags, conspicuous consumption, a love of gadgets and tech, cocktails and cars and well-cut suits.

And then Daniel Craig comes, and the world has changed again. The idea of masculinity has changed and Daniel Craig channelled that very effectively. That's the world my book is set in. An uncertain world. The rise of populism, increased polarity in political and social views, the proliferation of conspiracy theories, culture wars and ambivalence towards the state, a growing understanding and fear of climate change. As I say, nothing is certain anymore. We are living on shifting sands. Bond has to reflect that – while at the same time offering hope, like he always did. He will kill the dragon. Good will win over evil. The funny thing is some people have responded to this book in an affronted manner. They don't like being presented as the bad guys. Which makes me laugh.

Q: What is it like writing the villains for these books? How do you make it so that these colourful villains don't overtake the narrative?

A: Well, the character of the villain is perhaps the element in a Bond story that you need to work hardest on, because Bond is Bond. To an extent, he's always the same. The best films are the ones with the most memorable villains. You don't want them to become interchangeable Dr Evils. You don't want to just come up with a mad, strange foreigner with some physical disabilities. You need to try to come up with something new and distinctive, while, as with everything else, keeping them recognisable as Bond villains. I think, whatever you think of this book, Æthelstan, the villain, sticks in the mind.

What's interesting is that, since Fleming was writing the books and they were making the first films in the '60s, all these characters have emerged in the real world who seem to have based themselves on Bond villains – people like Putin, Trump, Kim Jong

Un and Osama bin Laden. They all have elements of the Bond villain and like to build themselves Bond-villain-like lairs. You've got to try and traverse that world. You've got to give the reader those familiar elements and try to put a twist on them.

Q: How did you tackle making the novel so inclusive?

A: I think Bond can still be Bond and do 'Bond things'. It's not something we need to get worked up about. Nobody is saying that men and women aren't allowed to sleep with each other. Bond is a secret agent, a superhero of sorts. He can drive fast cars, and he can shoot people if they've misbehaved. It goes right back to Fleming. He didn't bog the stories down with a lot of personal baggage. There are only tiny amounts of backstory in the books. There are moments where Bond is introspective, and he gets depressed and pissed off with what he's doing sometimes, but at the core of it, he's just getting on with it. A man on a mission. New books and films don't need to stray from that idea, and they're best when 007 is focused on the job in hand. You just have to make sure he doesn't behave like an arsehole. As long as Bond still does those 'Bond things' and gets on with his adventures, and we have fun following along, everything else is set-dressing, changing the curtains, changing the cut of his suits, changing the car he drives. If he stops smoking and shows more respect towards women, it's not the end of the world.

Q: When it comes to Bond, everyone's got an opinion about what's right or what's wrong. What are yours? Did you give yourself any rules and regulations?

A: I think he has to be a fantasy figure. A classic, resourceful loner who exists in the moment. He's not a real person. He acts out our own fantasies. He must never get married and settle down with kids. What other rules? I didn't want to get into the realms of default nasty foreigners. I didn't want to get into the realms of making the villains disfigured or disabled in some way.

Fleming himself felt that he was writing a very modern character. He was saying: 'The war has changed everything. We have to move on from cosy, lightweight crime thrillers featuring the likes of Lord Peter Wimsey. It's a nasty world and people do nasty things. He wanted to create a *protagonist* (he didn't consider Bond a hero) who was tough enough and cruel enough and resolute enough to occasionally do nasty things himself. This is James Bond. He's a fist. And when it comes to courtship he wants to get on with it. He has no time for flowers and dinner dates. Fleming would have been delighted by the relaxed sexual mores of the modern world. Women have as much agency as men. They can call the shots. If two young people want to go to bed with each other, there's no shame or scandal attached.

Fleming's Bond wants to move on from the stifling, rules-bound, tedious, old-fashioned system of 'courting'. Fleming is clear – men and women want to have sex with each other. Why do they have to go through six months of a lengthy social ritual leading up to getting engaged and then married before they can actually sleep with each other? Fleming was saying, 'Let's cut all that out, let's get on with it and do what we want to do.' He saw what Bond was doing in the books as quite modern and, in many ways, it was. But you look back on it now and it sometimes feels a bit brutal. So, I was trying to channel what Bond is but take out the aspects which really don't sit happily with modern readers. It's not a problem. You can do that and still keep Bond who he is at heart.

Q: You've made some changes from the hardback to the paperback edition of OHMSS. Can you talk us through your thinking behind that?

A: Somebody once said that a work of art is never finished only abandoned. And I tend to agree. Left to your own devices you could carry on painting a painting, or writing a book, for the rest of your life. But, at some point, you have to draw a line under it and say, 'It's finished. I'm done.' With every single one of my books, when it's come out, I've looked at it and thought 'Oh I wish I'd done this instead of that, I wish I could rewrite this part.' But you can't. Once a book is published, that's what it is. Although, of course, many books will go through updated editions if they last long enough.

As we talked about before, OHMSS was written in a crazy rush of energy. I was really happy with the result, but there was one part that always bugged me. As I mentioned, there's a framing device in the book – the beginning and the end are set on May 4th, two days before the Coronation, when Bond is trying to figure out who wants to assassinate the King. At the time of writing the book, in March, I had no idea what Charles would be doing on that day and where he might be. So, I came up with what, I have to confess, was a bit of a fudge. Bond is with Charles at an event, but we're never told exactly what the event is, or where it's taking place. Like Fleming, I love setting my stories in real places and putting in real detail. Fleming said, 'Why would he have Bond stay at the Porchester Hotel and not the Dorchester?' It was only after the book came out that we had more information about what Charles was doing in the run up to the Coronation.

Because I thought it was fun to have the opening of the book set on the day of publication and not on the day of the Coronation (and just in case something extraordinary happened at the Coronation that wouldn't get a mention in the book), I thought I couldn't set these passages in Westminster Abbey. But when I found out that there had been several full dress rehearsals for the actual event, I felt that one of them would work very well for the story.

I asked IFP and they were happy for me to make some changes. So, the opening and closing chapters are now set in Westminster Abbey, during the rehearsals for the Coronation. I was able to visit the Abbey and work out where the action would take place. It seemed a very fitting location, as Westminster Abbey is the graveyard of kings. There are 30 British monarchs buried there. So now we have a specific place and a specific event, and I can sleep easy. The other change I made was to put Bond in a classic 007 tuxedo in the big party scene that's central to the book. I'd resisted it before, and thought I'd try something different. But, Bond in full dinner dress is such an iconic image I knew I had to change it if I could. I also like the idea that he's in a room full of James Bonds, all the men are wearing tuxes. And, as readers will know, not all men look as good as James Bond when they're wearing black tie.

Q: What is your favourite Ian Fleming book?

A: I think his best-written, and probably my favourite, is *From Russia with Love*. It's the longest of the books. Ian half-jokingly said, 'This one's going to be proper book.' It was his last throw of the dice. The books he'd written had been successful in England, but he hadn't managed to crack America yet, despite the likes of *Live and Let Die* being set in the USA – a blatant attempt to get the Americans interested. He was before his time and he knew that unless he got films made of his books, which probably wouldn't happen until they took off in America, it would just be another parochial English crime series – a 1950s, black and white, Brylcreemed hair type of thing – and would be forgotten. He was really pushing right from the start to get Bond onto a bigger stage. And he put everything he could into *From Russia with Love*, to the extent that he actually kills Bond at the end of it – poisoned by the blade hidden in Rosa Klebb's boot – in case he didn't want to bring him back. Luckily, the book *did* do well, and once President Kennedy said he had it on his bedside table, it became a phenomenon. There was no looking back. Bond was brought back from the dead with a simple antidote. So Ian had really worked hard on that book and it's got some great writing and great characters. I think it's fantastic. Although, there are some sexual references and attitudes from one of the characters that feel off today. The sort of thing I was talking about before.

The Fleming books all have this quality... even if there are some moments that haven't necessarily aged well, they all have amazing passages and passages of brilliant writing in them that knock you out. *On Her Majesty's Secret Service* is one of the best. Some of the descriptions of skiing, which Fleming loved, are brilliantly, brilliantly done. He was a great writer of action. He could put the reader very much inside Bond's head. Oh, god, there are so many to recommend... *Casino Royale*, the very first, is a fascinating book because you can see the birth of Bond and you can see Fleming coming up with this idea and running with it. It's a great, tight little thriller. If you're going to start anywhere, either *Casino Royale*, *From Russia with Love* or *On Her Majesty's Secret Service*.

CHARLIE HIGSON

Charlie Higson is an author, actor, comedian and writer for television and radio. His Young Bond series began with *SilverFin* in 2005 and was followed by: *Blood Fever* (2006); *Double or Die* (2007); *Hurricane Gold* (2007); and *By Royal Command* (2008). All five novels entered the children's bestseller charts in the top five. His most recent book for adults is the crime thriller *Whatever Gets You Through the Night*.

IAN FLEMING PUBLICATIONS

Ian Lancaster Fleming was born in London on 28 May 1908 and was educated at Eton College before spending a formative period studying languages in Europe. His first job was with Reuters news agency, followed by a brief spell as a stockbroker. On the outbreak of the Second World War he was appointed assistant to the Director of Naval Intelligence, Admiral Godfrey, where he played a key part in British and Allied espionage operations.

After the war he joined Kemsley Newspapers as Foreign Manager of *The Sunday Times,* running a network of correspondents who were intimately involved in the Cold War. His first novel, *Casino Royale,* was published in 1953 and introduced James Bond, Special Agent 007, to the world. The first print run sold out within a month. Following this initial success, he published a Bond title every year until his death. His own travels, interests and wartime experience gave authority to everything he wrote. Raymond Chandler hailed him as 'the most forceful and driving writer of thrillers in England.' The fifth title, *From Russia With Love*, was particularly well received and sales soared when President Kennedy named it as one of his favourite books. The Bond novels have sold more than 100 million copies and inspired a hugely successful film franchise which began in 1962 with the release of *Dr No*, starring Sean Connery as 007.

The Bond books were written in Jamaica, a country Fleming fell in love with during the war and where he built a house, 'Goldeneye'. He married Ann Rothermere in 1952. His story about a magical car, written in 1961 for their only child, Caspar, went on to become the well-loved novel and film, *Chitty Chitty Bang Bang*.

Fleming died of heart failure on 12 August 1964.

www.ianfleming.com

🐦 TheIanFleming

📷 Ianflemings007

f IanFlemingBooks

National Literacy Trust

Changing life stories

The National Literacy Trust is an independent charity working with schools and communities to give disadvantaged children the literacy skills to succeed in life.

Our mission is to improve the reading, writing, speaking and listening skills of those who need it most, giving them the best possible chance of success in school, work and life. We run Literacy Hubs and campaigns in communities where low levels of literacy and social mobility are seriously impacting people's lives. We support schools and early years settings to deliver outstanding literacy provision, and we campaign to make literacy a priority for politicians, businesses and parents.

Visit literacytrust.org.uk to find out more, donate or sign up for our free email newsletter. You can also find us on Facebook, Twitter and Instagram.

DISCOVER
WHERE
BOND
BEGAN

www.ianfleming.com

The James Bond Books

Fiction

Casino Royale
Live and Let Die
Moonraker
Diamonds are Forever
From Russia with Love
Dr No
Goldfinger
For Your Eyes Only
Thunderball
The Spy Who Loved Me
On Her Majesty's Secret Service
You Only Live Twice
The Man with the Golden Gun
Octopussy and The Living Daylights

Chitty Chitty Bang Bang

Non-fiction

The Diamond Smugglers
Thrilling Cities